Pursuit of Honor

Forthcoming Books by Joseph O'Steen

A King's Pirate
Passage to Santander
Madras Command
The Emperor's Gift
In the King's Service

Pursuit of Honor

By

Joseph O'Steen

JADA

Pursuit of Honor

Published in 2004 by JADA Press
Jacksonville, Florida
www.JadaPress.com

ISBN: 0-9761-1109-8
LCCN: 2004117678

Printed in the United States of America

Our most grateful thanks to Captain Gary Bergman for providing *the beautiful photo of the replica ship Royaliste used on the cover of this book.*

The Royaliste is a 71' OA gaff-rigged, square-tops'l ketch refit to specifications of an 18th-century dispatch gunboat/bomb ketch.

Eastern Campaign: *The Royaliste* had a long and successful Eastern Campaign under owner Vernon Fairhead: From 1992-2002 she represented the Canadian War Museum, under contract to the Canadian Navy to act as an historical representation craft. As an historic vessel she participated in many naval-battle reenactments including a voyage to Louisbourg, Nova Scotia, in 1995. During Captain Fairhead's ownership *Royaliste* was also used in historical documentary films shown on the Discovery and History channels. During the summer of 1997, *Royaliste* sailed Lake Champlain, where she engaged in a re-enactment of the famous battle at Fort Ticonderoga.

Ensigns: She has flown the colors of 3 nations: France during the French Indian War, Britain at the start of the Revolutionary War and the United States during the Revolutionary War and the War of 1812. Now under new ownership, *the Royaliste* is patrolling the waters of San Francisco Bay under US colors. She is presently berthed at Pelican Harbour, 200 Johnson Street, Sausalito, California.

For special events the Royaliste also travels overland on short notice.

Visit the Royaliste and see how you can help her keep sailing http://www.privateerinc.org and www.theRoyaliste.com

Author's Notes

I have attempted to present action packed novels with the Nathan Beauchamp of the Royal Navy series of books. Although I have concentrated on the things I love in this genre of book (human aspects of life at sea coupled with broadsides and boarding actions) I am sure some age of sail enthusiasts will find the lack of sail handling and some of the other aspects of ship handling to be missing the degree of detail they are accustomed to. I have designed the series to serve as an entry-level primer for those who are beginning to wet their feet in this genre.

It is my hope that with these books I am able to introduce new fans to the age of sail in the Napoleonic Wars at Sea.

I would like to extend my appreciation to those who have assisted me with this project through their many contributions of support and assistance. Debby Blevins, Sheldon Levy, Karen Thompson, Barbara Mill, Christina Langston, Simon Nobbs, James Goddard, Aaron Yost, Captain Gary Bergman of the Tall Ship Royaliste, nautical author John Stevens, George Jepson, lover and seller of tall ships books and so many more who have encouraged me to write these books.

To my foster Father,

Edmound U. O'Steen,

who rescued me when I needed it most

and inspired me to be the person I am today.

Though our character is
Built from our experiences,
We should not steer by the
Wake of our past but
Rather navigate by the
Stars in our future.

...Author Unknown

Contents

Prologue

In the early 1700s an escaped slave of African royalty turned to piracy. For several years he roamed the Florida Keys attacking ships of all nations. He called himself Black Caesar. Black Caesar was skillful and vicious in the pursuit of his chosen trade. He later joined the pirate Blackbeard and sailed north on the 40gun ship *Queen Ann's Revenge*. In September 1718 near Ocracoke Island off the tip of Cape Hatteras, British Naval Lieutenant Maynard successfully attacked the *Queen Ann's Revenge*; Blackbeard is killed. Black Caesar is captured and taken to Williamsburg, Virginia where he is hanged.

On Friday the 13th in July of 1733 the annual Spanish Treasure Fleet of 22 ships sails from Havana, Cuba for Spain. The next day a hurricane swept all but one ship to their destruction. The sunken ships are scattered over 30 miles of the Florida Keys. The Spanish government salvaged what treasure they could over the next few years however, millions of pesos remained on the bottom of the shallow waters of the Florida Keys.

Nearly one hundred years later a man of mixed blood arrives in the Florida Keys. He takes the name of Black Caesar and resumes the pirate trade of his namesake. His attacks on innocent ships are deadly and he always leaves one survivor to spread the word of his deeds until the mere mention of his name causes ships to surrender or flee.

In late 1803, word reaches London that this Black Caesar has discovered the wreck of the Spanish Treasure ship *San Pedro* in the shallow waters between Lower Matecumbe Key and Indian Key. It is learned that Irish Rebels, who intend to use their share of the treasure to wage a revolution on the British Government, are financing the salvage operation with Black Caesar.

The British government knows that while at peace with Spain a naval squadron cannot be ordered into Spanish territory to stop Black Caesar and his Irish benefactors.

The Admiralty is directed to devise a plan for a clandestine venture to prevent the pirate and the Irish Rebels from succeeding in recovering the treasure and arming the Irish Rebellion.

A former Dutch merchantman is taken into the Royal Navy, armed, and outfitted as a pirate raider. Commander Nathan Beauchamp is given command and ordered to the Spanish Florida Keys to prevent the San Pedro's treasure from falling into Irish hands.

His Majesty's pirate ship *Hawk* sets sail on an adventure of danger, romance, mutiny and the "Pursuit of Honor".

Chapter One

HMS Hawk

Nate walked down the dark Admiralty corridor nearly skipping. Less than an hour ago he had entered Captain Culleton's office at the Admiralty to be reassigned to one of the ships in Britain's rebuilding fleet. He had entered the office a mere lieutenant, just recently returned from the Jamaica Station in the West Indies. Now he strode down the corridor as his Majesty's newest most junior commander in the fleet. *Commander Nathan Allen Beauchamp, Royal Navy.* He mumbled the title to himself, *but now I have my own ship; the HMS Hawk of 22 guns,* his thoughts caused him to smile from ear to ear like a lad in a sweets shop. *Well, at least she would soon have the guns, spars, powder, and sails,* all things that make a ship into an instrument of war.

His thoughts became much more serious as he pondered his orders to join *HMS Hawk* at the Portsmouth Naval yard and oversee her conversion from a clumsy merchant ship to a British man-o-war.

His walk slowed as he neared the door to the clerk's office and the assignment waiting room, where all the transferring officers came to receive their orders. He stopped, drew in a deep breath, pulled his uniform into proper place, stuffed his hat under his left arm and with his most official naval bearing, opened the door. Inside the room waiting lieutenants looked up, their eyes wondering why this young officer had been called to Captain Culleton's office. Nate walked briskly past the clerk's desk, dodging the pacing Lieutenant Porter who had just received his orders to command the sloop, *Ajax,* before Nate had been summoned to the same office. Nate smiled at Porter and acknowledged his look of curiosity with a brief nod of his head.

Stepping out of the Admiralty and down the steps, Nate rubbed his eyes to adjust them to the bright sunlight, and stared straight into his Brother James' face. "James!" he exclaimed as they embraced. "How did you know I was in London?"

James pulled back from the embrace and took Nate's hand, shaking it as his older brother never had before. "Nate you are a grown man," releasing Nate's hand and sizing him from top to bottom. "It is amazing what a little time and fresh sea air will do to change a boy into a man." James placed his arm around Nate's shoulder and began guiding him across the street to a nearby pub. "Captain Culleton sent word as soon as he heard you were in Portsmouth," James guided Nate around a puddle from the morning's rain. "He said you would be rushing to London to get your new orders."

Nate pulled his head back slightly to better see James' face. "But James, why are you here in London?"

James nodded his head toward the White Lion Pub. "Lets take a table in here and I will tell you," he held the door open and urged Nate through. "I'm afraid I have some bad news."

Nate gazed back over his shoulder to see Jasper, standing on his tiptoes attempting to peer over the traffic in the street. He nodded for Jasper to stand fast with the luggage and then turned to James once more. "What kind of bad news, James?" He followed as James weaved through the crowded pub. "It must be terrible news for you to come all the way to London."

James looked around the crowded room. "In a moment, Nate," he then saw who he was searching for and raised his hand to get the attention of the serving girl. Evidently his signal was prearranged as the girl began pushing her way through the other patrons and led them to a private room at the back of the pub.

He pulled out a chair from under the table and indicated for Nate to do the same.

After Nate had settled into his chair, his brother reached across the table and took Nate's folded hands in his own. "Nate, as the youngest brother I know you were close to father."

Nate sprung up from his seat. "James! Has something happened to father?" Tears trickled down his cheeks as Nate braced himself for the worse.

The older brother took a deep breath, glanced down at the table then back up to look Nate in the eyes. "Yes, Nate. Father had an accident on his ship, at Portsmouth, last month."

Nate leaned forward listening for the words he dreaded to hear. "How bad was he hurt, James?"

Sliding his chair back, his brother walked around the table and placed his arm around Nate. "He was killed, Nate."

He was weak in the legs and he felt faint, then his knees began to buckle. His brother caught him, eased him into the chair, and poured a glass of claret. Then placed it in his hands and guided it to his mouth. "Here, Nate, take a drink. It will calm your nerves."

With one gulp he downed the drink then wiped his mouth on his sleeve. Through green eyes clouded with tears he looked at his older brother. "How did it happen?"

James took another deep breath, sharing Nate's pain. "A falling block, while they were stringing some new cables." Nate's heart was heavy with great sorrow; then he thought of another who would hurt more than he. "How is mother?"

James sat back down across from Nate, adjusted his cuffs, and then brushed some spilled claret drops from his sleeve. "She took it very bad at first." James poured himself a glass. "She is much better these days but misses him terribly." James poured Nate another glass of claret.

Nate downed another drink and stood up, brushing his uniform coat with shaking hands. Then, drying his eyes on his sleeve, he looked at James. "I must go to her."

James stood, finished the last of his drink, then went ahead and opened the door for Nate. "Do you have any leave coming?"

They pushed their way through the crowd of men in the pub's main room. Nate raised his voice as the two brothers approached the front door. "I don't have more than a few days before I have to report to my ship."

They stepped out onto the street and saw Jasper had moved his and Nate's luggage to in front of the pub. He sat on Nate's sea chest patiently waiting.

The glaring noonday sun made Nate's eyes squint. He turned back to James and gestured in Jasper's direction. "This is Jasper. He is my...er, well we don't know what his position is to be but, he is in my employ and will be coming home with us."

James reached across Nate to offer his hand. "Please to meet you Mr..."

Jasper stood and accepted James offered hand. "Beauchamp," he smiled from ear to ear, exposing his ivory white teeth set in his dark black face. "Jasper Beauchamp, at yo'r service, Sah!"

James tilted his head and rolled his eyes up at Nate in a most questioning way.

Nate smiled and slapped him on his back. "I'll have to tell you about that some day."

*****

The carriage raced down the country lane, drawing ever closer to the Beauchamp estate and Nate's home. He could hear Jasper laughing as he and the driver joked about some unknown subject atop the coach's driver's seat. He watched out the window as the countryside changed, becoming more familiar with each passing mile.

James broke the silence for the first time in the last hour, and said, "That little fellow, Jasper, seems to be attached to you."

Nate looked over at his older brother then back out the window as the coach raced on. "Yes, I suppose he is," he smiled to himself. "He owes me for his freedom and I owe him for my life." Then glanced back to see James' puzzled expression. "I rescued him from some bounty men in Kingston, and then he joined the *Falcon's* crew." He stretched his head out the window and gazed forward to get a bearing and judge how far from home they might be. The brisk air ruffled his dark black hair back from his face. *Not far now*, he thought. He pulled his head back in to the coach. "I'm sorry, James. Where was I?"

James smiled at Nate's eagerness to get home. "Jasper had just joined the crew of the, *HMS Falcon."*

He retrieved his handkerchief from his pocket and wiped the road dust and perspiration from his forehead. "Oh yes," he continued. "We were after the French privateer Roseau," he unfolded the handkerchief, looking for a clean spot, and then wiped the rest of his face. "We found him in Fort de France, Martinique, on a vessel we were cutting out," He glanced out the window again then back at James. "Roseau had the best of me in a sword fight. I slipped and fell to the deck," he folded the handkerchief and placed it back in his pocket. "Roseau was making his downward swing to finish me off when Jasper killed him." Nate stared through the coach window at nothing in particular. "Yes, we owe each other what we each hold dearest," he spoke with sincerity. "Jasper, his freedom, and me, my life." Nate turned and smiled at his brother. "A fair trade. Would you not say?"

The coach slowed to make the sharp turn into Rockshire's driveway. Nate gripped the coach door handle and peered out the window. The driver slowed, letting the horses cool down as they neared their destination. Slowly the coach passed the monuments of his childhood. The fields where he played, the hill he and Joseph had built their fort on to fight dragons and Vikings, and finally the stable where he and Virginia Crampton would sneak away from his brothers to talk of the future days when he would be a great sea captain like his father, and she would wait patiently at home for his return.

The driver leaned down and shouted at the window. "Rockshire, Sirs. Looks like you have a welcoming committee awaiting you." The coach took a sudden turn left then stopped at the front steps of the great house.

Nate did not wait for the driver to pull out the coach's steps. He flung open the door and leaped to the ground then raced up the steps to his waiting mother and brothers, Nathaniel and Joseph.

"Oh, Nathan," Beatrice Beauchamp cried his name. She held him tightly to her bosom, then reached up placing her hands on his strong shoulders and pushed him out to her arm's length to get a better look at him. "You have been gone such a long time." She pulled him close again for a tight hug. "You were so young and small when you left and look at you now, so grown." Nate smiled at the Spanish accent his mother never overcame.

Joseph and Nathaniel gathered round them, all hugging Nate. "Look at you now," Joseph smiled at his younger brother. "A commander. Why, you have caught up with me." They all stepped back to look up and down at him in his commander's uniform. Joseph placed his arm around Nate's back and walked him towards the front door. "I had better get busy or you will pass me and make post captain before I do." They all laughed and Nate and his mother went into the house. His brothers followed closely with Jasper and Edgar, their butler, close behind, carrying Nate's sea chest.

The next two days were spent visiting with his family. They talked of things past; fond memories of his childhood and of his father. Nate brought them up to date on his life and career in the navy. They told him of their lives while he was away and discussed their future plans. Joseph would go back to his North Sea squadron, James would continue to manage the estate, and Nathaniel would continue as a barrister in Falmouth. Beatrice was growing more accustomed to a life without her husband but talked of visiting her ancestral home in Minorca, Spain. Much of Nate and Joseph's time was spent attempting to convince their mother that it was not safe to travel abroad in these times of war.

On the third afternoon Nate received an invitation for dinner at the Crampton's home, *Southgate*. He bathed while Jasper prepared his best dress uniform.

Arriving at Southgate promptly at seven in the evening as the invitation had indicated; Nate was met by Squire Crampton. "Ah Nate, my boy, how good of you to come."

"My pleasure, Sir. I am honored to see good friends after such a long time," Nate replied.

Squire Crampton stepped aside and motioned for Nate to enter the house. "Dinner will be ready in a few minutes. Shall we step into the library and have a sherry while we wait?"

"I would be delighted, Sir Nigel," Nate followed Sir Nigel down the hall and into the library. As they stepped into the library Nate reminisced, *I have been in this house many times as a child but have never been in the library. The library had always been a secret place where adults met to conduct business with the squire, now I have been invited.* He grinned at how time and age had changed things for him.

Sir Nigel went directly to his wine cabinet, pulled a bottle from the top shelf then retrieved two glasses from the bottom shelf. He poured a generous portion in each glass and handed the first to Nate, then took the other and nodded toward two stuffed chairs near the garden door. "Nate, I have wanted to talk to you for a long time."

Nate raised an inquiring brow. "I have been away for quite some time, Sir."

Sir Nigel took a long drink of his sherry then placed the half empty glass on the table beside his chair and leaned forward towards Nate. "I have been following your career through friends in the service." Sir Nigel smiled warmly and patted Nate's knee. "Lad, I have a business offer for you." He stood and walked to the fireplace, opened a box on the mantel and took out two pipes and a pouch of tobacco. He held out a pipe to Nate who shook his head, declining the offer. Sir Nigel replaced one of the pipes, then packed his own with a fragrant blend of tobacco. Reaching down, he retrieved a small stick from the fire and lit his pipe.

Drawing in the smoke as he puffed his pipe to life, he walked back to his chair and continued, "As you know, I have some very successful shipping concerns." Stooping to look for acknowledgement in Nate's face and satisfied that Nate concurred with his success, he continued, "I own more than twenty fine merchant ships," using the tip of his pipe to point to a beautiful ships model on the mantel near the tobacco box.

Nate nodded his head in agreement. "Yes, Sir, I am aware of your business success, but I do not know what that has to do with me."

"Nate, I will get right to the point," Sir Nigel rose from his chair once more and paced the open area between the chairs and the fireplace, somewhat like a naval captain on his quarterdeck. He seemed to be searching his inner self for the correct words. Swinging around and pacing back towards Nate as he began to speak again. "Nate, I know you are fond of Virginia and she is coming of marriage age," he stopped and took a different tact. "Should you decide to quit the navy and marry Virginia, I would be pleased to offer you command of the *Mary Louise,* my finest ship."

"Sir, I am honored," Nate stood and approached Sir Nigel. "I am very fond of Virginia and may very well ask for her hand some day, however, I have a career with the navy which I find quite satisfactory."

"Come, now, Nathan," Sir Nigel exclaimed. "You are the sixth son in the Beauchamp family!" He excitedly attempted to persuade Nate to accept his offer. "Surely you can not expect any inheritance. You will only have your navy pay to support yourself and any future wife and family."

Nate was growing tired with this conversation but did not wish to offend Sir Nigel. There was only one way to end the discussion without accepting the offer. "Sir Nigel, it is an attractive offer, particularly with my feelings for Virginia, however, I will require some time to consider the offer," he turned as he felt a presence enter the library doorway and then continued. "I must leave for my ship in the morning. I will think on your kind offer and inform you of my decision in the near future."

"Sir, dinner is served," Hamilton announced from the doorway.

"Very well, Hamilton." Sir Nigel reached his hand toward Nate and beckoned him to follow. "Nate, I will accept that for now," he motioned for Hamilton to proceed. "I am quite sure an intelligent young man, like yourself, will make the correct decision." Sir Nigel followed Hamilton down the hall. "I am absolutely famished! How about you, Nate?"

*****

The coach rounded the bend in the road and pulled past a stand of trees. Nate sucked in his breath and emitted a low whistle at the site down below in Portsmouth Harbor. For as far as he could see the mast of ships preparing for war lay anchored in various stages of readiness. Somewhere amongst that forest of masts lay the *HMS Hawk* and his task to make her into a King's Ship.

As the coach wound through the bustling streets of Portsmouth to the navy yard, the wondrous sights of a city filled to the brim with the commerce required to rebuild a nation's navy filled Nate's eyes and mind.

Such a sight was seldom seen on this magnitude as merchants and shopkeepers mixed with warrant and commissioned officers, eager to sale their naval stores. Freight haulers with their wagons filled with naval stores, line, chain, canvas, pitch and tar as well as thousands of other items required to build and support the fleet, coaxed their teams of horses through the human mass towards the naval yards.

Street urchins dashed about between horses' hooves and wagon wheels dodging the tips of the whips wielded by frustrated wagon masters struggling to get their supplies to their destinations on time. Seamen staggered from inns and taverns with ladies of opportunity clutching their arms. There seemed to be chaos and noise coming from every direction and mixed into this was the stale smell of human habitation and horse manure.

He leaned on the coach's windowsill staring at the crowds of people and shook his head in wonderment of the strange site, then mumbled to himself. "Looks like ants at an outing."

The coach slowed then came to a stop in front of the marine sentry post at the naval yard. Nate leaned his head out the coach window and asked the sentry. "Corporal, which way might I find the *Hawk*?"

Before the sentry could answer someone among a group of seaman unloading a nearby wagon yelled out. "*Hawk*, here? Not likely. This here yard's for real navy ships not merchant ships!" The working party burst into laughter.

Nate flung the coach door open and jumped down, his boots crunching on the gravel as he strode swiftly toward the seamen.

"Here, now you men mind your manners and get back to work." A young lieutenant chastised the seamen and walked to where Nate stood angrily watching. "I apologize for the men's remarks, sir," he turned to glare at the seamen then back to Nate. "I am Lieutenant Foster, Howard Foster." He and Nate walked back to the coach where Jasper now stood with a walking stick in his hand. "May I help you, Sir?" Foster asked.

Nate pointed to the empty seat next to the driver. "That won't be necessary, Jasper, climb back aboard." A calmed down Nate extended his hand to Lieutenant Foster. "Thank you, Lieutenant. I was merely trying to find where the *Hawk* might be." He looked back at the working party of seamen. "Evidently she is not too well thought of in these parts."

Lieutenant Foster tried not to smile. "There are so many purpose built navy ships being taken out of ordinary that the common seamen tend to look down on converted merchant ships." He motioned for Nate to follow him as he stepped outside the naval yard gate and pointed down the road. "You will find the *Hawk* and several other ships undergoing conversion about five miles down the road in Mr. Sarris' yard." Nate's eyes followed Foster's pointing hand with disbelief. Continuing, Foster said, "There are so many ships that the naval yard is over flowing." One look at Nate told Foster that more explanation was required. "Mr. Sarris is a Greek from up north somewhere. The Admiralty has hired contractors to come to Portsmouth and set up yards to help get the fleet built up for the war."

The young commander shook his head and started walking back to the coach. "Thank you, Lieutenant Foster." And climbed into the coach. "Driver, turn the coach around and take her down that east road, about five miles," he glanced back at Foster. "You have been most helpful, Mr. Foster, I thank you."

Foster walked with the coach as it turned around. "Glad I could be of assistance, sir." The coach pulled past the gate and turned east on the road. Foster trotted along side the coach. "If you are in need of a good officer, sir, I'm on the receiving ship and readily available."

Nate nodded to the young officer as the coach's increasing speed left him standing alone on the dusty road.

*****

Nate and Jasper stood on the quay, Nate's sea chest and Jasper's sea bag at their feet, watching the coach disappear through the gates to Mr. Sarris' shipyard. Suddenly they felt lonely, strangers in a strange place. They turned around to look at their new home the *HMS Hawk*. Nate just stared.

She was tall and wide like the Dutch ships he had passed at sea. She sat high in the water indicating her capability of carrying large cargos across deep waters.

Jasper was the first to speak. "Cap'n, dat don't look like no naby ship. She look mo lak a pirate ship!"

Nate drew in a deep breath. "No, she certainly doesn't look navy, does she Jasper?" He straightened his hat and slapped at the dust on his uniform. "Get your sea bag, Jasper, I'll send someone for my chest." They started down the dock heading toward the ship. Nate stared up at her bulwarks as they came abreast of her. *She looks like a double deck ship of the line, only lacking their length.* He turned and walked up the loading plank to the main deck. "Well, Jasper, we have three months to make her into a navy ship."

Jasper smiled his famous smile that always seemed to make things better, "Oh, yes sah, if'n we all can whop up on pirates n frenchies we sho kin make dis ship a naby ship."

Nate stepped onto *Hawk's* main deck and was nudged out of the way by two yard workers carrying lumber up the boarding ramp. "Watch yer self, lad, dis here ain't no loaf o bread we be carry'n," the lead man said as he passed by heading toward and then down the main hatch.

Nate felt a tugging from under his feet then glanced left to see a seaman pulling at the rope he was standing on. The seaman spoke as Nate stepped aside freeing the rope. "Pardon, sir, if I don't get this line coiled and put away the first officer will have my hide."

Nate nodded his understanding to the seaman. "By all means carry on."

The seaman smiled a gap toothed smile and continued rolling the line in a great coil on the deck. "Thankee, sir."

"By the way," Nate interrupted the seaman once again. "Just where might one find the first officer?"

The seaman continued to coil the line but nodded his head in the direction of the main hatch. "He were help'n da carpenter, last I see'd him."

Nate, closely followed by Jasper, stepped over to the main hatch, grabbed the ladder sticking high above the hatch combing and backed down into the hold with Jasper following shortly afterward. They stepped into a beehive of activity. Hammers and mallets clanged and saws echoed off the ship's interior as they ripped through freshly cured lumber, a smell Nate remembered from Squire Crampton' s lumber mill back in Falmouth. An officer, in shirtsleeves only, leaned over a group of men who were banging some sort of brace against the aft bulkhead.

"That's it, Mr. Hughes," the officer stood up and patted the man he was talking to the back. "I think that will do quite nicely, at least until we get more lumber cut." He grabbed a cloth from the saw table and wiped his hands. Turning to leave he saw Nate and Jasper. "And just who might you be, sir?"

Nate gazed around at the activity in the ship's hold. "I'm Commander Beauchamp. I've been ordered to take command of the *Hawk.*"

The officer stepped forward and saluted. As he did, the watching workmen ceased work and stood staring at the two officers and the black man. "I am sorry, sir, we did not expect you for a few more days." He turned to the watching workmen and instructed them, "Carry on men, there is lots to be done in a short period of time." Pointing up the ladder he said, "We may speak better on deck, sir." Following Nate up the ladder, he looked around at the crowd of workmen on the deck and recommended, "We had better step over to the quay so we can hear each other and not be heard."

Nate and the first lieutenant walked down the loading plank and traveled a ways down the quay, escaping the noise still heard from the *Hawk*. The first lieutenant introduced himself, "I am Lieutenant Abraham Kent, your first officer. At your service, sir."

Nate shook the first lieutenant's hand. "Happy to meet you, Mr. Kent." Taking a moment to size up his new first lieutenant he decided that he liked what he saw in him; he had a competent air about him. He stood just a few inches shorter then six feet tall, with light brown hair, which was lightly bleached by the sun suggesting that he wasn't afraid to work outside to get a job done. He had clear sky blue eyes placed into a long face with a firm jaw. Nate looked back to the *Hawk;* "Now, what is all this construction about?"

"Mr. Kent! Mr. Kent!" An older, stocky man with graying hair came running down the loading plank and rushed up to the captain and first officer as fast as his short legs would carry him. He excitedly interrupted them as he drew near. "Sir, that ship is a cow!" He was red faced and out of breath when he looked back at the *Hawk*. "That ship will never be a king's man-o-war!"

Mr. Kent placed his hand on the old man's shoulder to calm him and get his attention. "Mr. McClain, this is Commander Beauchamp, our captain."

The old man drew deep breaths realizing his unprofessional demeanor. "Beg pardon, sir."

Mr. Kent smiled at the excited old man and introduced him to the captain. "Sir, this is Mr. Ezra McClain, our Sailing Master."

Nate offered his hand to the master. "I take it that you have inspected the ship, Mr. McClain?"

"Aye, sir, I have," Mr. McClain tried to conceal his embarrassment by looking at the ground.

Nate waited for the master to look up again, and then preceded, "You have an opinion, Mr. McClain?"

"Aye, Sir," Mr. McClain's attempt to hide his distain for the ship failed as he spilled his opinion of the ship to the captain and first officer. "You can not have honor with this ship, sir. She is under canvassed, has no draft to speak of, rolls like a barrel and sits too high in the water for her guns to bear at close quarters, except for a frigate or better." He shook his head in the negative. "We will not be able to out fight a cutter with this cow."

Mr. Kent patiently waited for the master to finish then pulled him closer to himself and the captain. "I was about to inform the captain so I may as well tell you also since you will be heavily involved in the work." He glanced around to assure no one was within earshot and continued. "A few days ago I received specific orders on how the *Hawk* is to be converted," he looked up once more then back to his audience of the captain and the master. "She is to have the normal nine-pound guns on her deck but we have been ordered to reinforce the lower deck to take twelve pounders."

Nate studied Mr. Kent's words; "The Admiralty must have a special assignment in mind."

"I'd say so, sir." He glanced back at the curves of the *Hawk's* sides. "The instructions say to make the gun port doors flush and paint them the same color as the hull." He looked back at Nate; "You have a pouch from Captain Culleton of the Admiralty in my quarters, sir."

Nate started walking back to the *Hawk*. "I'll read them as soon as my sea chest is taken to my cabin."

Kent informed Nate, "I'm sorry, sir. Your cabin is in disarray and will not be completed for another eight to ten days." He stood aside to allow Nate to board the loading plank first. "You could have my cabin, sir."

Nate walked up the loading plank and stepped aboard the *Hawk*. "That will not be necessary, Mr. Kent, Jasper and I will take rooms at the George Inn." The thought of Jasper brought an idea to mind. "Mr. Kent, have we a servant on board?"

Abraham Kent mentally went over the ship's roster. "No, sir. I don't believe we do."

Nate nodded toward Jasper. "I should like this man rated Captain's Servant in the ship's roster."

Chapter Two

Pirates and Rebels

Nate rolled up a blanket and placed it on top of the hard wooden bench to soften the seat. He drug his newly modified captain's chair over to the long table in the *Hawk's* gunroom and continued to review the ship's logs and records in spite of the pans rattling and singing coming from the galley. He smiled at Jasper's attempts at seaman's shanty songs and hoped his cooking would fair better than his singing.

He had been looking through the ships books for nigh on four hours and the old bench was taking its toll on his aft equipment. He stretched his arms and back, then rolled his head around to get the kinks out of his neck and for what seemed like the first time, he looked around the gunroom. He thought, *this must have been one of the Hawk's first cabins modified for naval use.* It was cavernous by most naval standards. The individual cabin's canvas walls, like all ships of war, were so designed so they could be removed during battle to allow the gunners more room to fight the ship. These walls extended from the larboard side out to perhaps eight or nine feet and seven feet fore n aft. By far the largest cabins he had seen on all but the largest ships, and those were in the East Indian merchant fleet. The starboard cabins were a mirror image of the larboard cabins. He counted sixteen canvas cabins. *Several more than any normal ship with a commander as captain,* he thought, then nodded approval to himself; *no matter who they were, there would be no complaints from the officers about their accommodations on this ship.*

Normally a captain would never enter the officer's sanctuary without first being given permission, however, these were extenuating circumstances. One deck above the gunroom sat the captain's cabin which was cluttered with new drums of paint, tar, pitch, lumber and other items required for transforming the old merchant ship *Hawk* into a man of war. The shipyard's plan called for the captain's cabin to be the last part of the ship modified, something about special appointments for it. Nate questioned, *what is so secret that the captain cannot be told what the plan for his ship would be?* He reached under the arms list and pulled out the orders from Captain Culleton's office.

He read the inscription on the front of the envelope.

> *"To: Commander Nathan A. Beauchamp, HMS Hawk."*
> *"From: Admiral Sir George Montague"*

He ran his fingers over the words as if to make sure the ink would not rub off making his promotion merely a dream. The thought made him smile. He carefully lifted the flap to the envelope containing his first set of orders as a commanding officer, pulled them out and began to read, once again, dwelling on what he thought to be key points.

You are to report to Portsmouth and immediately take command of HMS Hawk. You are further required to assure the instructions for her conversion are followed to the letter. Upon the completion of the lower deck, you are to dismiss the yard crew. You will embark the officers, ship's crew and warrants as they are assigned by this office with the exception of two officers and one midshipman of your choice. There will be 312 men and officers including one marine major, one sergeant major and 32 marines. This ship's company will be comprised of British citizens of natural and foreign descent. You will then move the ship to Fishbourne on the Isle of Wight where you will complete the conversion with the assigned compliment of the Hawk's ship's company.

You will take whatever measures necessary to assure that no naval or military officer, nor any civilian is permitted aboard HMS Hawk under any circumstances. The accompanying letter explains that you are under Admiralty orders that take precedence over all other orders concerning you and HMS Hawk. This letter may be shown to validate their priority.

When you deem the Hawk is up to naval standards, you will take on stores for an extended voyage; then notify this office; then await further orders.

Admiral, Sir George Montagu
Commander-in-Chief
His Majesty's Royal Navy
Portsmouth

Nate stroked his fingers across his chin as he studied the orders. *Three hundred and twelve men to man the Hawk.* He opened the flap and slid the orders back in, then placed the envelope in his right hand desk drawer, drew the key from his vest pocket and locked the desk. *How mysterious, what kind of mission would require us to have so large a crew?*

A knock on the gunroom door startled him from his thoughts. The door opened slightly with Lieutenant Kent's head poking through the opening. "Sorry to disturb you, sir, but this letter just came for you." Kent looked around the gunroom as if assuring the captain had not changed anything. He settled his eyes on Commander Beauchamp to find him waiting patiently for the letter Kent held out in his hand. "Oh! Sorry, sir, I thought it might be important."

Nate took the offered letter turning it over to open it and saw the seal of Admiral Montague. He felt a presence and looked up to find Mr. Kent hovering in the same spot as if nailed to the deck but more in anticipation of some news his captain might share with him. "That will be all, Mr. Kent!"

Lieutenant Kent straightened with a slight shadow of disappointment on his face and turned to leave the gunroom.

"Oh! Mr. Kent," Nate slid the letter opener down the length of the envelope. "It seems our crew will be chosen for us by the Admiralty with the exception of two officers and a midshipman."

Lieutenant Kent turned half way back to face his new captain. "Isn't that a bit unorthodox, sir?"

"Exactly what I was thinking, Mr. Kent." He laid the letter opener down and pulled the contents from the envelope while looking up at his first officer. Pondering the situation for a bit, he then carried on. "At any rate it is up to us to choose the three," and glanced down at the still folded letter. "I know of a Lieutenant Howard Foster on the receiving ship at the navy yard," he lifted the top half of the folded letter and looked back to Mr. Kent. "He should do nicely if he is still of a mind to join us." He opened the folded letter, spread it on his desk and began to read then stopped when he realized he had left the young lieutenant waiting. He smiled. "You choose the other two, Abraham. You don't mind if I call you Abraham do you Lieutenant?"

"No, sir. Well actually I go by Abe, if you don't mind." Mr. Kent's smile showed that he felt more at ease with his young captain.

"Good then, Abe, you may call me, Nate. That is when we are alone." He waved his hand at the gunroom around them. "We may need all the friends we can get before this voyage is over."

"Well sir, you may be right, but if I don't go fetch us a couple of officers and a midshipman we may never get started." They both laughed as Abe Kent departed the gunroom.

Nate continued to read the letter from Admiral Montague. *Looks like I'm going to a dinner party.* Nate pulled his new gold hunter from his vest pocket, flipped the cover open to see Virginia's portrait starring back at him. *Such a beauty, a man could do a lot worse than marry this beautiful woman and inherit a shipping company. I'll have to give Squire Crampton an answer soon.* He gazed at the watch face. *Almost noon and I have much to do.* "Jasper!" He yelled above the rattling pans in the galley. "Belay that mess and fetch us a coach. We have to get our dunnage to the George Inn."

Jasper came aft from the galley pulling on his blue jacket with its bright brass buttons. "I be's rat back, wid a carriage, suh!" He flew through the gunroom door and raced up the ladder to the deck. Nate smiled as he heard Jasper's light tapping feet scurry across the deck and down the boarding plank. *What would I do without that little man?*

*****

The coach driver pulled the team to a stop right in front of the George Inn's door. Jasper jumped down from his perch adjacent to the driver, pulled the steps out and opened the coach door for Nate. Nate had removed his sword and placed it on the facing seat so that his ride to the inn would be somewhat more comfortable. He stepped from the coach and reached back in to retrieve his sword. He fastened the sword belt around his waist and turned to step into the inn and bumped into someone's chest. His eyes were locked into the eyes of an older gray haired man with a bleached white complexion and cold blue eyes. The man was in some kind of fancy uniform. "Oh! Please excuse me, sir." He backed up to give the man a way to pass.

"That is quite all right, Commander." The man was in the uniform of a full admiral with all it's gold lace and buttons. With the admiral was a smallish, older, thin man with spectacles perched atop his long crooked nose. He was stooped over with what appeared to be a slight hump on his frail back. A smallish man with coal black eyes and puffy red cheeks followed them. Nate's eyes roamed from the admiral, to the man with the hump, to little red-faced man, and back.

He stiffened his back and gave the admiral a salute. "I am sorry, sir." He returned his saluting hand to his side and stepped farther back to allow the three gentlemen room to pass. "I was not watching where I was going, sir."

"Nonsense, Commander, we were engaged in conversation and not aware of your presence." The admiral patted Nate's elbow as they passed. "Good officers are alert to their surroundings at all times," the admiral smiled. "That makes you and I both at error."

Nate and Jasper watched the three men walk down the street until they turned at the first intersection. Jasper was the first to move as he approached the inn's door, which he opened for his captain. Nate stepped through the entrance to find the innkeeper smiling.

"You are indeed lucky, Commander," the Innkeeper said as he returned to behind his desk. He reached in the box behind him and drew out two keys. "Normally Lord Jarvis would have given you a right proper dressing down," passing Nate the room key, "This one is for yourself, sir," he shifted a larger key from his palm down to his fingers and reached it out for Nate to take. "This un be for your man," he said, and pointed in the direction the inn's back door. "There is a room at the top of the stairs above the stable."

Nate took the larger key and passed it to Jasper and turned back to the innkeeper. "Lord Melville?" Sounding a bit surprised Nate exclaimed, "You don't mean the First Sea Lord, the Earl of St. Vincent?"

"Aye, that I do." The innkeeper smiled and pointed in the direction the admiral and the little stooped gentleman had walked. "He and the gentleman stay here every time they are in Portsmouth."

Nate nodded his head as he gazed in the direction the innkeeper pointed. "And who is the man with the First Lord?"

"That would be Commodore Fry, he always accompanies the First Lord when he visits." He retrieved his guest ledger from in front of Nate, glanced at it assuring his newest guest had properly signed and placed it under the counter. "I heard some say he was in the spying business." His eyes searched around the lobby. "Reckon that is why he does not wear a proper uniform." He beckoned a young man from his seat near the door. "Rodney, give this officer's man a hand with his baggage."

Nate glanced back to where he last saw the First Lord and the crooked little man. "Why would the First Lord travel with such a man?"

*****

Nate read the invitation's address then looked up the long drive at the well-lit house with all the people coming and going. Carriages full of people arrived and empty ones pulled out the gate and stopped along the street to await the passengers' return from the admiral's dinner. No doubt, this was Admiral Montague's home. He turned in the gate and moved up the long drive. A coach rattled behind him and he stepped to the side to let it pass. The light from the torches along the drive reflected on the window of the coach as it passed. Nate gazed on the loveliest alabaster face he had ever seen. The young woman brushed a bright red curl of hair from her face as the coach passed. As he continued his walk up the drive he watched the coach stop and the passengers disembark. A short, thin man, in a dark green suit was the first to emerge from the coach. The man immediately turned to assist the woman as she took his hand and stepped down. She wore a beautiful light blue dress and Nate could see when she lowered the hood of her dark blue cape that the dress complimented her fair skin and flaming red hair. The man retrieved a long black cane with what appeared to be an ivory lion's head handle from the coach and they disappeared past the doorman into the admiral's home.

The coach pulled away from the door as Nate approached the home's entrance. The doorman's round red face filled with a smile as he briefly inspected Nate's invitation and waved Nate to enter. From where Nate stood in the receiving line, he could see the man in the green suit shake the hand of a senior naval captain while the beautiful redhead curtsied. They exchanged pleasantries and moved on to Admiral Montague. Nate's position in the receiving line moved ahead slowly. He watched as the admiral took the man's hand in his right hand while patting his shoulder with the left. The man in the green suit moved on and the admiral embraced the young lady, smiling as best he could with what appeared to be a mouth full of replaced teeth. Nate arched his eyebrow, they must be well known to the admiral.

"Good evening, Commander Beauchamp, so glad you could come," a voice called to him as he felt his right hand being pulled and shaken by a young lieutenant.

He snapped away from his thoughts of the young couple to stare into the lieutenant's face. "Good evening, lieutenant," he briefly gazed in the direction of the admiral but found the young couple had disappeared into the crowd. "When the admiral calls, one had best come. Would you not say, lieutenant...eh?"

"Jack Barnes, sir." The lieutenant introduced himself and nodded towards the admiral. "Flag Lieutenant to Sir George."

"Good to meet you, Lieutenant Barnes." Nate glanced to see the captain patiently waiting for him. "Looks like I am holding up the line." Nate moved on towards the waiting captain.

"My friends call me Barney," Lieutenant Barnes raised his voice slightly above the noise in the foyer.

Nate reached his hand to the waiting captain and spoke over his shoulder to the lieutenant. "My friends call me Nate." He returned his attention to the captain.

"Commander Beauchamp, I am Flag Captain Martin Thompson." The captain pulled Nate from the line of guest. "We have been waiting for you." Captain Thompson tapped the admiral on the arm and motioned to Nate. "Admiral, this is Commander Beauchamp."

Admiral Montague nodded and whispered something to his wife.

Captain Thompson leaned toward Nate to be heard over the noisy voices in the receiving line. "The Admiral wishes to speak with you before dinner." Then straightened up, and motioned for Nate and Lieutenant Barnes to follow him.

Nate and Barney followed Captain Thompson into the admiral's library. He glanced back to the chattering guest in the receiving line to see Admiral Montague excuse himself and follow the three naval officers.

Admiral Montague entered the library and came over to shake Nate's hand. "My home is a noisy place tonight, eh, Commander?" He pointed out a stuffed red chair in front of his huge oak desk. "Take a seat, Beauchamp." Sir George walked behind his desk and pulled out his chair after nodding to Lieutenant Barnes to close the library door. "Be seated gentlemen and we will tell Commander Beauchamp what his mission is all about." Sir George sifted through a stack of papers on his desk. While riffling through the papers he glanced at Nate. "I am sorry to hear of your father's death. Achilles Beauchamp was a fine officer and my particular friend," he looked through the papers again. "He shall be surely missed by his friends and the navy."

"Thank you, Sir George," Nate adjusted himself in the overstuffed chair. "That is very gratifying coming from such an accomplished officer as yourself."

The admiral pulled the paper he sought from the pile. "Ah! Here it is." He spread the paper in front of him and smoothed the edges while he gathered his thoughts. "I suppose you have wondered what all the mystery is about with the *Hawk*." He half smiled and studied the paper resting in front of him.

"It has been somewhat unorthodox so far, sir."

"Commander, Britain has a potential problem that we think you and the *Hawk* can assist us with." Sir George glanced at Captain Thompson for conformation.

Captain Thompson pulled his chair closer to Nate and the admiral's desk. "Commander, first let me tell you some history, then we will get to the root of our problem and your mission." He went to a cabinet behind Sir George and retrieved a chart, returned to the admiral's desk and spread the chart, placing the admiral's inkbottle and whatever else was available on the edges to keep the chart from rolling back up.

Nate leaned forward and briefly studied the chart. "Spanish Florida, the Keys to be exact."

"Correct, Commander," Sir George nodded to Captain Thompson to proceed.

Captain Thompson commenced his briefing, "In the early 1700's an escaped slave of African royalty turned to piracy. For several years he roamed the Florida Keys attacking ships of all nations." Captain Thompson settled back in his chair and continued with what appeared to be the beginning of a long story. "He called himself Black Caesar. Black Caesar was a skillful pirate and vicious in the pursuit of his chosen trade."

The captain reached for the wine decanter on the admiral's desk, held up the bottle, and Nate nodded his acceptance of a glass. Lieutenant Barnes appeared with four glasses and poured a round for the four officers.

All the while Captain Thompson's history lesson continued. " Black Caesar later joined the pirate Edward Teach, Blackbeard, as we know him. Black Caesar sailed north with Blackbeard on the 40gun ship, *Queen Ann's Revenge.*"

Captain Thompson sipped his wine, sloshed it around in his mouth and swallowed. "That is mighty fine Madeira you have, Sir George."

Sir George developed a sheepish grin. "Yes, even we admirals can appreciate what the revenuers let the smugglers slip through their hands."

"Right! Now where were we?" Captain Thompson rubbed his forehead to help stimulate his memory. "Oh! Yes, a few years later," he rubbed his head once again. "Somewhere near 1717 or was it 1718, well it matters naught, the *Queen Ann's Revenge* was near Ocracoke Island off Cape Hatteras in the Carolinas; Blackbeard was killed by navy Lieutenant Maynard and this Black Caesar was taken to Williamsburg and hanged."

Captain Thompson took a deep breath and held his glass for Lieutenant Barnes to refill, as did Nate and Sir George.

The captain took a long drink of his Madeira, set his glass down and leaned over the chart of the Florida Keys. "On Friday the 13th of July in 1733, the Spanish Treasure Fleet of twenty-two ships set sail from Havana, Cuba." He turned and smiled at the young commander. "The very next day the fleet was struck by a devastating hurricane that swept all but one ship to destruction, spreading them over thirty miles of the Florida Keys." Taking a quick sip of his wine, he ran his finger over what Nate assumed to be the area of the Keys where the wrecked ships lay.

Captain Thompson waved off the offer of a refill from Barney and eased back in his seat. "Millions of pesos were scattered in the shallow waters of that thirty miles of Florida Keys." He pulled at a loose thread on his navy blue coat, lost in thought for a moment, and then he slid forward in his seat and looked directly at Nate. "In the 1730s, the Spanish salvaged part of the cargos of hides, spices, gold, silver and jewels, however; many of the wrecks and millions of pounds of treasure have never been found."

"That is not until now," Sir George piped up as if he had been waiting his turn to speak.

Nate and the other two officers gave the admiral their undivided attention and interest.

"It seems Black Caesar has returned and located the treasure ship *San Pedro*.

"Sir, that is impossible," Nate stood before he realized where he was. He sat back down clutching the chair arms. "When I was stationed in the Caribbean I heard stories of this

Black Caesar." He glanced sideways at Barney and Captain Thompson for concurrence. "Like Captain Thompson just said Black Caesar was hanged almost a hundred years ago."

Sir George smiled at Nate's confusion. "That is correct, Commander." Pulling another paper from the drawer of his desk, he said, "I have reports that a man of mixed heritage has appeared in the Keys and taken the name Black Caesar." The admiral leafed through the new papers and slid out a single, weathered sheet. "This report is from the governor of the Bahamas, it appears that this Black Caesar has resumed the career of his namesake." Sir George ran his index finger down the page stopping at a paragraph, which he quickly scanned, his lips forming the words as he read to himself. "The new Black Caesar or Black Caesar Two, if you will, has been attacking innocent ships with a deadly force and he always leaves a single survivor to tell of his atrocities against the crews and passengers." The admiral stacked the papers and laid them aside. "He has created a fear in the local shipping concerns that has adversely affected commerce between the mainland of Florida and the Caribbean."

"Admiral, why don't we join with the Spanish and capture or drive this pirate out of the Keys?" Nate queried.

"Commander, we shall tell you the rest of the information we have and how you and the *Hawk* fit in to our plans." The admiral stood, moved around his desk, and sat in the chair next to Nate. "Commander, we have reports that tell us that Black Caesar is well financed by Irish rebels who intend to use their share of the treasure to fund a rebellion against the crown."

"I see, sir," Nate slipped back in his chair and digested the ramifications of what the admiral had just said.

"We are not at war with Spain so we can not send a squadron into Spanish territory and we certainly are not in favor of the Spanish increasing their treasury but most of all we can not let the Irish rebels get any of that treasure." The admiral stood and placed his hand on Nate's shoulder. "So we have devised a plan to create our own pirate ship to deal with Black Caesar and the Irish."

Nate looked up at Sir George. "I take that it is the *Hawk* you are referring to, sir?"

"Yes, Commander Beauchamp, it is you and the *Hawk* that will take this mission to Spanish Florida for your King and country." Sir George returned to his seat behind the desk.

"Sir, the *Hawk* is a lumbering, old Dutch merchantman, she is slow, wallows in the seas and sits too high in the water for her guns to bear." Nate stressed his point and waited for the admiral to agree.

"I am aware of her sailing qualities," Sir George took an intake of air and pondered his next words carefully. "I was not prepared to tell you this commander until the modifications to the *Hawk* were completed." He picked up his quill and ran the feather through his fingers several times before he spoke again. "When the modifications are completed and you have taken on stores, you will take the *Hawk* to Fishbourne on the Isle of Wight, as previously instructed." He motioned for Lieutenant Barnes to fill all the glasses with another round of Madeira. "There you will be met with a hoy carrying sixteen twelve pound canon; they are for the lower deck Mr. Sarris' yard has been strengthening." The admiral smiled like the cat that had just captured a mouse. "That should make the *Hawk* sit lower in the water for you."

Nate nodded his head in agreement. "Those Dutch merchantmen are known to be slow under sail, sir."

"It is the responsibility of each captain to obtain top performance from his vessel, Commander." Sir George slid his chair back and stood. "I'll not expect any less from you, sir."

Nate stood as the admiral and the other officers walked toward the library door. "I'll do my best, Sir George."

"I am sure you will, Beauchamp," Sir George nodded for Barney to open the door. "I should attend my guests now; Lieutenant Barnes will introduce you to your dinner partner."

Nate silently mouthed, "Dinner partner?" to Barney as the admiral departed the room.

Barney pushed Nate's chest to stop him until the admiral was out of earshot. He grinned as he informed Nate, "Mrs. Montague likes for her guest to be paired off," he chuckled. "Must be the matchmaker in her."

"What am I paired with?" Nate asked. "Likely some spinster from who knows where?"

"Not exactly. She has appointed you to Mrs. Hiram Harper." Barney was enjoying Nate's predicament.

"Mrs. Hiram Harper!" Nate was taken aback. "Hiram Harper is a full captain in command of a third rate."

"Yes, he is," Barney chuckled. "But he is away at sea and she needs an escort for this evening."

Nate looked down at the floor in disappointment.

Barney took Nate's arm and guided him into the dining room. "You do not wish to upset the admiral's wife, do you?"

Nate realized the consequences and sheepishly followed Barney to his assigned place at the table where Barney indicated for him to sit. He nervously adjusted his silverware and watched the gaily-dressed people up and down the table. It was evident that many of the people knew each other. He felt like he was on a deserted island while here in the middle of all these people he did not know, then he saw the redhead near the end of the table on the opposite side. She and the gentleman in the green suit were seated near Admiral and Mrs. Montague. Her beauty was breath taking, never had he seen such a striking woman. *I'll have Barney introduce us after dinner.*

He felt a tugging at his right elbow and turned to where Mrs. Harper was assigned to sit. She was middle aged yet not unattractive. Her wig was of the latest French design, curled atop her head in white swirls. Her eyes told of a slightly tired woman who may have attended one too many parties. Her white dress too was of French design, cut low in the front, exposing more than he would expect a woman of her age and station in life to reveal in public. He realized he was staring at her bosom and snapped his head up to hear her engaged in conversation with him. "I am sorry, Mrs. Harper, I'm afraid my mind was somewhere else."

"I noticed that, Commander Beauchamp, and I am flattered." She smiled a warm smile at Nate and he felt his face blush.

He ran his fingers around the inside of his collar, either trying to let more air in or just from a nervous habit, he was not sure which it was. "I am quite sorry, Mrs. Harper, but you are so lovely tonight," Nate attempted to placate the woman.

"Oh, I am not offended, Commander," she wrapped her arms around his and snuggled into his side. "I am quite flattered. Perhaps you will see me home after dinner." Mrs. Harper rubbed Nate's leg, smoothing a wrinkle that had materialized when he seated himself. "Portsmouth can be a very dangerous place after dark and I would feel so secure with a naval officer to escort me."

Nate pulled at his collar again and looked around the table to see if anyone was watching as Mrs. Harper draped herself all over him. Luckily everyone was too involved with his or her own doings to notice, that is except Jack Barnes, who sat across from Nate grinning from ear to ear. He could see no way out except to volunteer to see Mrs. Barnes home; so he agreed, and Mrs. Barnes pulled away as dinner was served.

He looked down the table at the redhead to see her looking in his direction. Even from this distance he could see that her eyes were like blue crystals twinkling in the reflection of the candelabra directly in front of her. She smiled and turned to speak with the admiral just as Mrs. Harper dropped her napkin. Nate bent over and retrieved it and as he rose up Mrs. Harper took the napkin and slowly tucked it between her breasts and fluffed it out to cover her dress. "Thank you, Mr. Beauchamp."

"My pleasure, Mrs. Harper," Nate leaned sideways toward her as the waiter placed fresh pork on his plate.

"Please call me, Sarah, Commander," she cooed in his ear as she pushed her breast into his arm.

Nate adjusted his collar once again and felt his face burn with embarrassment. Barney grinned across the table and sipped his wine. Nate mouthed the silent word "Help," to Barney, hoping for some reprieve that would prevent him from escorting Mrs. Harper home. Barney got up and walked around the table and tapped Nate on the shoulder nearest Mrs. Harper. "Commander Beauchamp, I should remind you, sir, that Admiral Montague desires you to return to your ship before the next tide."

Nate turned to Mrs. Harper. "I am so sorry Mrs. Harper, I had totally forgotten. I'm afraid the lieutenant is right, I must return to my ship or face the admiral's wrath."

Mrs. Harper's face turned to a frown. "But Mr. Beauchamp, you promised to see me home after dinner."

"I am so sorry, Mrs. Harper." Nate laid it on thick. "A sailor's duty is first of all things." Standing, he pushed the chair back and stepped out beside Barney, "You of all people can appreciate that, I'm sure."

"Well, er yes," she swung back to face the table, adjusting her blouse as she did, "I suppose I can, perhaps another time Commander."

Nate and Barney stepped quickly to retrieve Nate's hat. He glanced back to his seat at the table and saw Mrs. Harper had already dropped her napkin between her and the gentleman on her right. Nate smiled at Barney. "I owe you a great favor for rescuing me, Barney."

Barney shook his head in the negative. "No bother Nate, you may do me the same service someday."

They both laughed as they proceeded to the front door.

Nate stopped to look back. "Say, Barney, who is the redhead next to the admiral?"

Barney glanced back at the far end of the table. "Oh, that is Barbara Hayes, the admiral's god daughter. Her father was the admiral's first flag captain," he turned and took Nate's hat from the servant. "She and her brother, William, are just in from Dublin," handing Nate his hat he continued, "They are in the shipping business and are in Portsmouth to board one of their ships for a voyage abroad on some family business."

"Ah, then the gentleman in the green suit is her brother," Nate smiled to himself. "You will have to introduce me sometime."

"Not much chance of that dear friend." Barney guided Nate towards the door. "You are leaving soon and they are leaving tomorrow."

"Perhaps when we all return." Nate stared at the end of the table until the admiral's doorman closed the door.

"Shall I summon you a coach?" Barney pointed to the line of parked coaches along the street.

"It is damp tonight; I think I would appreciate that."

Chapter Three

Women

He rolled over on his back and sank down in the large feather bed, a luxury he was not afforded on a King's ship. The thin cot, aboard ship, had never the less always been a welcomed comfort for overworked sea officers. His bones ached and his head throbbed from a slight over indulgence of the fine Madeira at Sir George's party. He smacked his lips, mentally re-tasting the fine red wine. He rolled to his side and came to rest facing the window where a shiny bright beam of the morning sun struck his closed eyes like a saber of light, penetrating beyond his closed eyelids, into the very center of his groggy brain. He swung his numb body away from the sun's intrusion on his semi consciousness, scratched his head and rubbed his hand across his face forcing his wine tainted breath up his nose. The horrible odor caused him to shake his head in an attempt to expel the foul smell from his nostrils. He glanced around the room, getting his bearings, and then the idea hit him as if it were always there. Perhaps he had thought of it last night as he slipped into a tired, contented sleep or maybe the idea came to him in a dream, but at any rate it was clear in his mind now. *I have to see her again.*

Nate swung the covers aside, grabbed his trousers and hopped to the washbasin, pulling on his pants. He scooped water in his hand, took a sip, swished it around his mouth and spit it into the nearby can of convenience. He again held his hand over his nose and mouth to test his breath. His nose crinkled up and he repeated the process to clean his breath. *Well, coffee will take the bite out of it.* Nate shrugged. Tap! Tap! An awkward sound came from the room's door to the hallway. Nate grabbed a towel, wiping his face as he crossed the room. "Who is it?" Nate questioned.

"I's come ta give ya yer morn'n shave, sir." Jasper spoke through the door.

Nate swung the door oven to reveal a smiling Jasper juggling a steaming bowl of hot water and Nate's shave kit.

*****

He rushed down the stairs, grabbed a quick cup of coffee in the dining room while Jasper hailed a carriage. He rushed out the front door, snatching his hat from Jasper's outstretched hand and boarded the carriage. He shouted from the carriage window as it pulled away. "I shall return before dinner, Jasper." He glanced up to the driver then back at the bewildered Jasper. "Have our dunnage ready to return to the ship tomorrow morning."

Jasper shook his head from side to side and mumbled to himself. "Cap'n sho is in a hurry dis morn'n." He turned back to the inn's front door stopping to watch the coach race around the corner.

*****

Nate tapped on the forward wall of the carriage signaling the driver to pull over. They rolled to a stop near the corner, which led to a dock area where many of the merchant companies maintained shipping offices. He exited the carriage and paid the driver. The young commander pulled his coat into place while looking around. He gathered his bearings and determined he was at the beginning of the street where he had been told the shipping office was located. He stepped off in the direction of the Dublin West Indies Shipping Office, taking in the sights as he strolled down the cobblestoned street to the harbor. On his right was a row of shipping warehouses. He peered through the giant opened freight wagon sized doors of the first one he came to. A studying look down the open center of the warehouse revealed men busily loading several wagons with all the needed stores that England imported to keep her commerce going, particularly in wartime. He saw timber from the North Sea countries, sugar from the West Indies, indigo from the East Indies and bales of cotton from the southern region of the still new United States of America. He turned to continue down the street. *Americans, they seem so much like us.* His nose caught a familiar odor. *Tar and pitch! Now I wonder what country sends tar and pitch our way?* He looked through the open doors of each succeeding warehouse as he made his way down the wide street. Much the same activity was taking place in each of the warehouses. Materials either coming in or being loaded on hoys to go out to ships bound for the ports throughout the world.

It seemed like the natural way of things to Nate. *They send us their goods and we send them ours. Commerce, keeps the world going and this war makes it all the more important.*

He stopped in front of the last warehouse; the great wagon doors were closed. He lifted his hat and mopped his brow with his cambric handkerchief. "Odd," he said aloud. He looked back up the street to all the activity going on at the other shipping warehouses then once again to the closed doors. He backed to the middle of the cobbled street and looked up at what appeared to be a newly painted sign. His lips mouthed as he read the sign, "Dublin West Indies Shipping Ltd." He stepped over and tried the front door's handle, *closed.* He glanced up the street, then down to where the street ended in a quay as if he expected someone to step up and explain why a shipping office with a ship sailing today would be closed at this hour.

He pulled his coat aside, reached into his vest pocket, and retrieved his pocket watch. He flipped open the lid to check the time and there stared the lovely Virginia looking him dead in the eyes from her mini portrait. He guiltily snapped the lid shut then realized he did not see the time. *Never mind, I do not need to know the time right now.* He turned around to see a clock in the window of the arms shop on the other side of the street. He walked over to check the time and perhaps find an answer as to why the shipping office was closed on the day they were scheduled to have a ship sail. Nate glanced back at the newly painted Dublin West Indies Shipping sign. *Perhaps they do not open to the public till just before the ship sails.* He fanned his coat to release the morning heat and bring fresh air in to cool him. *Still they should be delivering their goods early to the markets before they open.* He turned back to the direction he was walking just in time to prevent him from walking into the arm's shop front window.

He bent over to see the hands on the small clock, *two bells, 9:30 in the morning*; he stood up and looked through the shop window. There she stood with a shop clerk, at the far end of the shop, looking at a wall of displayed swords.

He entered the weapons shop and stood for a few moments just inside the door, taking in the sight of this beautiful woman. Streaks of fiery red hair escaped from under a black tricorn hat with a white ostrich feather trailing downward from the back. She wore black riding trousers with a silver stripe down the legs and shiny coal black boots. A black bodice laced up over a very bright red long sleeve blouse.

Her animated conversation with the clerk was barely audible from where he stood. He took a deep breath and proceeded down an aisle with cutlery on one side and muskets and pistols of all fashion on the other. As he approached her and the clerk he heard them discussing the qualities of the various swords but his thoughts were on the lovely view of her bosoms. The black bodice pushed them upward while the blood red blouse accentuated them quite nicely. Nate smiled at the lovely sight, with amorous thoughts filling his head.

"I shall be with you in a moment, sir" the clerk awoke Nate from his thoughts. He realized he was staring at the young woman's chest.

He slowly lifted his eyes from her chest to her face and noticed tiny red freckles dotted the lovely alabaster skin of her face. "Actually, I stepped in to speak with Miss Hayes."

"Do I know you, sir?" She wrinkled brow and made a quarter turn away from Nate indicating she was aware of his wandering eyes.

"Er..." he stammered. "I saw you at Admiral Montague's dinner last evening but with all the comings and goings did not have a chance to introduce myself." He nervously fidgeted with his coat's white lapel. "When I saw you in the shop, I thought I would take the opportunity." Nate removed his hat and bowed slightly. "Commander Nathan Beauchamp, *HMS Hawk*, at your service, ma'am."

She relaxed her guard slightly and smiled. “Oh yes, I do remember seeing you at Uncle George’s.” Barbara Hayes extended her hand.

“Uncle George?” Nate questioned as he took the offered hand.

“Yes, well actually he is our Godfather. My brother, younger sister and I, that is.”

Nate nodded. “I see.” He bent slightly bringing her hand to his lips.

“How gallant you are, commander.” Barbara’s warm smile drew Nate’s attention to its beauty. “A fine example of naval gentleman.”

He beamed at the compliment while waving his hand at the array of swords hanging on the wall. “Admiring the cutlery?”

“No, Commander Beauchamp, I am buying one for my voyage,” Barbara Hayes once more surveyed the beautiful swords displayed before her. She shook her head at her indecisiveness. “There are so many to choose from that I’m afraid I am having a difficult time deciding which is best for me.”

“Perhaps I might be of assistance,” he stepped closer to the wall and removed a beautiful sword with a gold gilded dolphin pommel “This Toledo is a fine sword, made from the finest Spanish steel.” He gripped the handle and ran his fingers along the shank. “It will keep its sharp edge longer than most swords,” he handed Barbara the Toledo and continued as she parried it around, feeling the balance. “A straight sword, like this is a great ceremonial sword.”

She quickly handed the sword back for Nate to return to its display. "I'll not be needing a ceremonial sword, Commander Beauchamp." He wrinkled his forehead with disapproval as she scanned the other swords on the wall. "I'll need something to fight with...er...that is, should we run afoul of an enemy or say pirates. Why, I may need to defend myself."

"Please call me Nate, Miss Hayes." He studied the swords looking for just the right one which would most likely fit her needs. Something fairly small and light weight. One she could handle yet would provide her with protection should the need arise. Barbara followed Nate as he moved along the wall of displayed swords. He stepped forward and took down a curved sword with a ruby embedded in the pommel; it was surrounded by gold rope filigree. Nate balanced it on his fore finger. "This Wilkerson is the finest fighting sword made."

Barbara took the sword, felt its balance and standing in a fighting stance, sliced the air several times. "Thank you for you guidance, Nate." She turned to the waiting clerk. "I'll take this one. Please have it sent out to the *Castlebar* before noon."

Nate was unable to conceal his broad smile. "A wise choice, Miss Hayes, let us hope you never have need to use it in anger."

"Call me, Barbara." She smiled as she locked her arm with Nate's and guided him towards the front of the shop. "You never know when a lady must defend her honor."

A confident Nate was sure he had slipped into this young lady's life. "Barbara I would like to take you for a tea or coffee, if I may."

"I would like that very much." The bell on the front door of the shop dinged and they both snapped their heads to see who had entered.

A young woman rushed through the door, glanced left, then right before looking in the direction of Nate and Barbara. Her eyes lit up with recognition, then she quickly walked down the aisle toward them. She was dressed similarly to Barbara, black riding pants and boots with a black bodice but where Barbara wore a blood red blouse the young woman wore a powder blue blouse. She had fair hair and skin with a wide bright smile full of white teeth.

Barbara introduced the young woman as she approached, "Commander Beauchamp, this is my sister Christina."

Christina curtsied. "Pleased to meet you, Commander." She immediately turned to Barbara. "Thomas said to tell you that we must board immediately as the tide is beginning to turn."

Barbara released Nate's arm and hurried over to the clerk. "I had best take the sword with me, sir." She slid the sword into the scabbard and clasped the sword belt around her waist and headed to the shop door. She looked back before stepping into the street. "Please send the bill to the Dublin West Indies Shipping office across the street." She stepped through the door and looked back once more.

"Perhaps another time, Nate," then she was gone, the door slowly closed behind her.

Nate and the clerk looked at each other and both shrugged their shoulders at the same time. Nate stepped to the window and watched Barbara and Christina disappear through the shipping office door across the street.

*****

Feeling dejected Nate stepped down from the carriage and reached up to pay the driver his fare. *So close, yet so far, bad timing or just bad luck.* As he turned to go into the George Inn he saw Jasper rushing up to him with a troubled look on his face. "What is it Jasper? What is wrong?"

"Oh! Cap'n we be in a mess." Jasper kept looking back at the George Inn's main entrance. He grabbed Nate's arm and pulled him down the street and away from the inn.

"Jasper! Get a hold of yourself and tell me what this is all about."

"Cap'n, Miss Ginia is here an she be mad at you." Jasper peered around Nate's shoulder as if looking for the devil to emerge through the door.

Nate took Jasper's arms and pulled his head around to face him. "You mean, Miss Virginia Crampton?"

"Yes sar, Missy Cramdon, dat be da one an' she sho be madder 'n a hornet wid da nest knocked down."

Nate glanced at the door. "Did she say what angered her?"

Jasper pulled Nate a little farther down the street and peered at the door once more. "Well sah, somth'n bout she ain't no cow and can't be buy'd."

Nate pulled away from Jasper and walked to the door, hesitated, then pulled it open and walked through into the foyer. Jasper clung to his arm and peeked through the opening between his arm and body.

The first thing Nate saw was the innkeeper behind his desk. It was evident the man was nervously pretending to be busy with his paperwork. The innkeeper looked up as Nate approached then turned his head to the normally empty couch in the alcove just off the foyer. Nate's eyes followed the innkeeper's gaze. There sat Virginia Crampton, arms crossed just below her ample bosom. Her breathing was rapid and she steadily tapped her right foot. Nate could almost see steam rising from her.

The innkeeper started to speak but Nate waved his hand to quiet him. He stepped through the alcove's arch, Virginia snapped her head in his direction, then sprung to her feet. "Virginia," He called her name but before he could finish she pointed her finger and began almost screaming.

"Nathan Beauchamp, how dare you barter for me with my father like I was cattle!"

Nate backed up as she came on wagging her finger in his face. "But, Virginia, I," he could speak no more before she continued her verbal thrashing of him.

"I heard what you and my father talked about and I will not be traded for, bought or sold." She pushed her index finger into his chest, forcing him back a couple steps then quickly walked to the front door. She spoke over her shoulder as she jerked the door open. "Nate, I love you but I will not be discussed like cattle by you and father." The door slammed leaving Nate in a momentary stupor.

He stood looking at the closed door, letting her words seep in.

Jasper stood clutching the corner of the alcove opening. "Is you go'n after Miss Ginia, Cap'n?"

Nate rushed for the door, passing the watching innkeeper who stood with his mouth agape. He pushed the door open and stepped onto the street. Virginia's carriage was rounding the north corner taking her home. "Damn!" He removed his hat and slapped his knees with it. "She could at least let me explain." He put his hat back on and reached his arms out, shoulder high, in a questioning manner. "Women. Who can figure them out?" he asked to no one particular. He turned and pulled the door open, Jasper staggered forward from where he had been peeking out. Nate shouted at the little man, "Hail a carriage and get our dunnage loaded, we are returning to the *Hawk*." He stormed past Jasper to inform the innkeeper they were leaving and settle his bill.

Jasper removed his new round hat by the brim and scratched his head. "Gona be a long trip to da *Hawk.*"

*****

The horse hoofs clopped against the cobblestones as they gingerly pulled the carriage through the traffic of Portsmouth's congested streets, weaving their way to the Sarris Shipyard.

Nate leaned back and stretched his feet out. He drifted in and out of thoughts of every event that had taken place this morning. *Virginia actually believed I would accept her father's offer. That would indeed mean her father would be trading the command of his best ship to see his daughter married.* He shook his head, *No wonder she is angry.* He gazed through the carriage window; the streets were bustling with the activity of commerce. He could hear Jasper telling the driver some tall tale over the busy street's noise. He drifted back to the arms shop and the lovely Barbara Hayes. He smiled as his mind repeated her last words, *"Perhaps another time, Nate."* His mind's eye saw her and Christina pass through the door to the Dublin West Indies Shipping office.

A serious cloud of thought passed over him. *Why was the shipping office closed when all the others were open? Why would a legitimate shipping company be concerned only with an outgoing ship and not with ships bringing in goods for resale?* His brow wrinkled over as he studied the possibilities. *If they are not a legitimate shipping concern then, what are they about? Surely the admiral's godchildren would not be into any illegal activities.* He pulled an Irish pendent from his left sleeve*, Irish! Rebels, perhaps...no.* He pushed the thought aside. *Their father was a British naval captain for God's sake.*

Jasper leaned down from his perch next to the driver and shouted into the carriage window. "Almost dair, sah."

Nate nodded his acknowledgement, scooped up his hat from the seat, and pulled it on. *The Dublin West Indies Shipping Company is not my concern; my concern is having the Hawk put in shape for her mission.*

Chapter Four

Fishbourne

Commander Nathan Beauchamp, Captain of *HMS Hawk* stepped through the entry port onto her deck; a beehive of activity surrounded him. Men of all shapes and hues of humanity buzzed around the deck. Some loaded stores from wagons on the quay while others worked feverously on the rigging preparing the ship for sea.

Mr. Kent looked up from supervising the lowering of a pallet of beef casks into the hold to see his captain and his captain's servant standing at the entryway. He strode across the deck to greet the commander. "Welcome back, Captain."

Commander Beauchamp scanned the activity on the deck and in the rigging. "You have been very busy, Mr. Kent." He glanced down at the nearly empty provisioning wagons. "Looks like you have us nearly ready to move to our next anchorage."

"Next anchorage, sir?" Abe Kent questioned his captain.

"Is my cabin available, Mr. Kent?"

Abe backed to the side and swung his arm as if clearing the way to the captain's quarters. "Yes sir, the last decorations were just installed this morning."

Nate's eyebrows arched up in a questioning manner.

Kent cleared his throat...ahmph. "You had better see it yourself, captain." Abe nodded in the direction of the cabin.

The captain started towards the cabin then stopped. "Jasper, see to our dunnage, if you please." He then continued down the few steps and stopped at the landing in front of the cabin door. He looked back at Kent who remained silent but urged him forward by nodding his head toward the door. Nate turned the handle and swung the door wide open. "Oh my," he mutter aloud.

Plush rugs covered the deck; red velvet drapes hung over the stern windows, while beautiful paintings with gold leaf frames hung on the walls. Nate had not seen such opulence on a ship since he had entered the *Falcon's* cabin after taking her from the French pirate Roseau in the Caribbean last summer.

"Captain, I do not know why it is this way but Mr. Sarris had instructions from the Admiralty to do this." Abe Kent explained.

Nate moved to behind the glossy white desk accentuated with gold trim. "Close the door Abe and take a seat." He pulled out the green, padded leather chair and sat down. "I'll tell you of our mission and how we are to be His Majesty's pirates."

*****

Nate finished informing Abe of their orders and watched the young officer's jaw hang open in disbelief.

"I could never imagine such a thing, sir." Abe Kent shook his head in disbelief.

Nate pushed his chair back then moved aft to the red velvet drapes covering the cabin's aft windows. He pulled them to the sides and wiped condensation from the panes then gazed out at the diminished activities on the quay. "Looks like we nearly have all our stores on board."

"Yes, sir." Abe stood up from the oak chair with velvet cushion as he glanced around the plush cabin. "It will require some time to become accustomed to these pirate comforts." He smiled at the captain and moved to leave. "I will check the progress and make the ship ready to sail." He reached for the door handle. "The next tide will be at eight bells."

"That should provide us with enough darkness to assure we are not seen leaving the quay." Nate let the drapes fall back into place and stepped toward the desk. "Were you able to recruit Lieutenant Foster?"

"Yes, sir, he was quite relieved to get off that receiving ship." Abe returned to his seat near the captain's desk. "I was also able to recruit a

Lieutenant Sheldon Levy and Midshipman Daniel Edwards from the same receiving ship."

Nate stroked his chin; stubbles from the day's beard growth were beginning to sprout. "This Lieutenant Levy, do you know anything about him?"

"Yes, he is a former merchant captain who lost his ship to a French Privateer," Abe stopped for a moment searching his memory then continued, "The *Republique*, I believe."

Captain Beauchamp uncorked a bottle of claret, and poured it into two glasses. He passed Abe a glass then took a sip from his own. "Levy, that is not a common name in the Navy."

"No, sir, it is not." Abe took a sip and continued, "Lieutenant Levy is Jewish." He drained his glass and set it down. "There are not many in the Navy."

Nate poured them both another drink. "I have never known a Jew who was not a merchant or money lender, do you know why he is in the Navy and why he is not captain of another merchant ship?"

Abe shifted his feet; concerned that his captain was upset with the recruitment of Mr. Levy. "I asked him these questions, Captain. It seems he hates the French and thought he would have a better chance of revenge serving on a Navy ship." Abe set back in the velvet padded chair in front of Nate's desk. "His sister is married to a politician who helped him procure a position as master's mate on the *HMS Andromeda*, His Captain thought well of him and recommended him for the promotion board."

"But why does he wish to serve with us?" Nate queried.

"He has heard that we are bound for the Caribbean." Abe slipped forward in his seat.

Nate picked up a silver letter opener with what appeared to be an opal in the handle. He turned it in his hand examining the high quality of such an everyday device. "If he has an idea of our destination I am curious who else might know our secrets?"

"Don't know, sir." Abe slid back in the seat. "I did not know myself until you just told me."

"It appears that we have a mystery, Mr. Kent." Nate leaned back in his seat. "We will have to question Mr. Levy and see how he found out about our destination, even if it is only partially correct."

Both officers were startled at the sudden knock at the cabin door. "Enter," the Captain shouted partly from the shock of the interruption and partly to be heard over the deck noise of a ship being loaded with stores.

A young seaman swung the door open and timidly stuck his head just past the doorway and knuckled his forehead in salute to his new captain. He stood staring, mouth agape, at the interior of a cabin the likes he had never seen before.

"Well, out with it, man!" Nate regretted his shouted words as soon as his lips released them. Few seamen had ever seen a cabin like this one and certainly naval ships had no cabins to match this opulence.

The seaman removed his stocking cap and crunched it with both hands. Gathering courage he spoke, "Sir, Master McClain sez ta tell ya that there is a Frenchie at the entryway claiming ta be the new second officer."

Commander Beauchamp and Lieutenant Kent shared a bewildered look. "Tell Mr. McClain to send down the Frenchman with his orders."

"Aye sir," The seaman donned his stocking cap and reached for the door.

"Wait!' Nate stood at his desk. "That accent, you are not British, are you lad?"

The seaman stopped with the cabin door halfway closed, his nose poking around the edge. "No sir, I am American." He paused slightly. "I am from Charleston in South Carolina."

"I thought so by the manner of your speech." Nate sat back at his desk. "What is your name lad?"

The nervous seaman snatched off his cap and nervously crunched it in his sweaty hands. His eyes followed the door as it slowly drifted open. "Robert Mantell, Topman, sir," he stuttered, then smiled "But my friends call me Bobby."

"Well, Bobby Mantell, carry my message to Mr. McCain, if you please." Nate smiled at the nervous Topman.

"Aye, sir." Mantell leaned over and grabbed the door handle pulling it to as his eyes wandered around the cabin for one last look.

Abe Kent leaned on his captain's desk. "Looks like the Admiralty is serious about handing us an international crew, Sir."

"How so, Abe?" Nate questioned.

Abe pointed his thumb towards the main deck where the workingmen could be heard rattling in several languages as they prepared the ship for sea. "Well, sir, so far we have been sent French royalist, Greeks, Italians, Spanish, some of those trouble making Irishmen and even a Moroccan."

Nate sat stiffly in his chair. "Yes it does, Abe." He picked up the letter opener and tapped it on the desk. "We will soon see what they have sent us for a second officer."

*****

Nate studied the tall slender officer as he approached the desk. The hair billowing out from under his tricorn hat was so black it seemed to have a blue tinge to it. His long thin nose rose from his face above an even thinner mustache. His high cheekbones and hollow cheeks sat on either side of blood red full lips that seemed out of place on such a thin, pale face. He carried a large scar that traveled from his jaw bone upwards through his patch covered left eye and terminated at his hairline. The man looked out of place in his British Lieutenant's uniform. The Frenchman snapped to attention and presented himself. "Lieutenant Louis La Rue, late of His Majesty's Royal French Navy."

Captain Beauchamp arched his eyebrows at Lieutenant La Rue's last statement.

Lieutenant La Rue, sensing the captain's displeasure with his reference to the Royal French Navy, continued. "Currently assigned to the British Royal Navy to fight the Republicans who have stolen my country."

Commander Beauchamp stood from his desk and extended his hand to welcome his new Second Officer. "Welcome to the *Hawk,* Mr. La Rue." He waved his arm in the direction where Abe sat sizing up the *Hawk's* newest officer. "This is our First Officer, Mr. Kent."

Lieutenant La Rue turned to face the rising first officer who offered his hand. "Welcome aboard, Mr. La Rue, I'm sure you will find the *Hawk* much more comfortable than your last assignment."

La Rue took the offered hand giving Mr. Kent a cursory shake. "But this is my first ship in your navy, Monsieur Kent."

Abe released La Rue's limp hand, arching his eyebrows in a most questioning manner at his captain.

La Rue dove his hand in his breast pocket, retrieved his orders and passed them to Commander Beauchamp. "My orders Monsieur Captain."

"Thank you, Lieutenant." Nate stepped around his ornate desk, placing his hand on La Rue's shoulder as he guided the new second officer to the door. "Have your personals taken to the gunroom. Mr. Kent will be with you shortly to assign you a cabin and determine your watch station." He patted the Frenchman on the back as he nudged him through the door. "Happy to have you with us, Mr. La Rue." Nate closed the cabin door and spoke as he returned to his desk. "Most curious that the Admiralty should send us a first time serving officer as second officer, don't you think, Abe?" He lifted his glass and drained the remaining claret.

Nate unfolded La Rue's orders and scanned down the page. All seemed in order, normal orders sending an officer from one assignment to another. His eyes stopped on the signature of the authorizing officer, Commodore Godfrey Frey. Nate looked up when he recognized the signature. *Why would the British spymaster be assigning officers to ships? Most curious.*

Abe stood looking at the closed door. "Most curious, sir." He turned back and set his empty glass on the corner of the desk, glanced at the door once more then back at Nate before continuing. "I had looked forward to recommending Mr. Levy as second officer, sir." He retrieved his hat from the opposite corner of the desk. "His experience would be a great asset to the *Hawk.*"

Nate shuffled the papers on his desk then stacked them to the side. "I am quite sure you are correct, Abe, but we must play the cards sent us by the Admiralty." He lifted the letter opener and stared at the inset jewel, deep in thought.

"If you will excuse me, sir, I will tend to getting Mr. La Rue settled in." Mr. Kent looked at Nate for concurrence.

Nate glanced up at the interruption of his thoughts. "Very well, Abe." He found himself tapping one of the Jack Tar tunes with the letter opener. "Let me know when you are ready to get the ship under way." As soon as the words escaped his lips he regretted reminding Abe of a task he knew would be standard for the first officer. He covered his nervousness to reassure Abe. "I am sure we will be able to utilize Mr. Levy's experience as third officer."

Abe turned back slightly, smiling as he pulled the cabin door open. "I'm sure we will, sir." He stepped through the door and called back to his captain. "We should be ready to put to sea within the hour, sir."

Jasper poked his head through the pantry door, his dark black face hidden except for the whites of his eyes and the shiny white teeth of his ever-present smile.

"Yor dinner be ready, Sah."

The *Hawk's* Captain looked up as his servant and friend approached carrying a crystal goblet and silver bowl on a large silver tray. He nodded at the desk top. "I'll dine here at my desk tonight, Jasper."

Jasper sat the tray on the desk then uncovered the silver bowl. He used the bowl lid to fan the rising aroma into Nate's face.

Nate wrinkled up his nose at the strange smell. "What in the world is this, Jasper?"

"Dems chitlins, sir." Jasper gave Nate one of his famous carefree smiles.

"What in the world are chitlins?" Nate's wrinkled nose in an attempt to stop the flow of the strange smell.

"Take a bite, Capt'n, you'll likes em." Nate took a small portion on the end of his fork and placed them in his mouth while Jasper continued, "Back on Master Rolle's plantation we dare not throw out anything wes' could eat so we learnt to make chitlins." The smiling Jasper leaned forward, watching Nate chew on the chitlins. "Capt'n ain't dem da best hog inners you ever had?"

"Hog Innards?" Nate gulped as the portion he had swallowed attempted to swim back up his gullet. "Just what do you mean hog innards?"

"You knows, Capt'n, The inside parts what run from the stomach to the...."

Nate held up his hand to stop Jasper from continuing, He fought the urge to spit the remaining portion he still chewed back into the silver bowl, just barely swallowing it instead. "Jasper, I am sure I will acquire a taste for...these...er chitlins, given time...I am not really hungry right now, just bring me a cup of coffee, if you please." He slowly pushed the tray from directly in front of him to the other side of the desk and quickly filled his glass with claret then gulped it down, swishing the foul chitlins taste away as he swallowed.

Jasper shook his head slowly from side to side. "I'm sho you gonna like chitlins soon enough if'n ya keeps try'n em." He lifted the tray and headed back to the pantry. "I'll jus eat des if'n ya don't mind capt'n."

"Be my guest, Jasper." Nate scrunched up his mouth thinking of what had just been inside, "Jasper, don't forget the coffee." He looked up to make sure Jasper had his back to him then he wiped his tongue on his sleeve, something he had not done since childhood. "And make that coffee strong."

Jasper shuffled towards the pantry, sniffing the chitlins and mumbling loud enough for Nate to hear. "Don't know how you 'spects ta be a pirate fo da King if'n ya don't eats good vittles."

Nate smiled at the little man even though the foul smell lingered on his breath.

*****

Commander Nathan Beauchamp, Captain of the *HMS Hawk* stood forward of the ship's wheel, his hand on the quarterdeck's starboard rail. He glanced up at the billowing sails as they filled with the land breeze that blew down the Portsmouth River. Still she did not glide across the small waves like most Navy ships, Instead her heavy bow ploughed through them. Her weight and ploughing effect provided for a smoother ride but reduced her speed to an almost embarrassing five knots. Nate patted the rail. "Old girl, you will really slow down when we get our armament on board." He scanned the sails once more, looking for ways to trim the sail to coax more speed from her heavy hull. *Not much we can do to the sails to gain more speed.* "Perhaps we can shift some stores to lift that bow some, might give her a knot or two."

"You say something, Captain?" the approaching Mr. Kent asked.

"No, Abe, just thinking out loud," he turned in Mr. Kent's direction. "What do you know about the *Hawk*, Mr. Kent?"

"You can see V.O.C. carved on the lower end of the mainmast down in the hold." Kent glanced past Nate, watching the lights of the anchored ships of His Majesty's Fleet slowly slip by as they made their way toward Gilkicker Point. He continued, "I asked Mr. Sarris what it meant and he said that he knows the ship, he has even made repairs on her. It seems she was built in '83 as a Dutch East Indian; the V.O.C. stands for Vereenlgde Oostindrische Compagnie, United East Indies Company. She was stationed in Batavia. The Company was dissolved in '93 and the *Hawk* was sold to an Irish Company who used her to trade with the Spanish and Dutch Islanders in the Caribbean."

"So she is a twenty year old veteran." Nate stared forward to lights shining seaward from Gilkicker Point. "Most of that time in southern waters." He turned back to Kent. "That is the hardest kind of duty for a ship and her wooden bottom. I hope Mr. Sarris paid particular attention to her bottom."

"She has had new copper on her bottom, I saw that when I first arrived."

"With so many ships coming into the service and so little wood available I hope Mr. Sarris has done her bottom justice and replaced any wormed or rotten wood." Nate nodded to the unlighted lanterns swinging in the rigging. "May as well get the lights lit, Mr. Kent." He glanced aft to the anchored fleet of Navy and Merchant ships they had just passed. "I think our departure was not observed and we do not want to be run into while crossing the Solent."

Abe Kent stepped to the larboard rail and pointed as the evening lights were lit, one by one on the old structure sitting on southern point of Portsea Island. "South Sea Castle, sir."

Nate joined Abe where both men leaned on the cap rail to take in the sight of the ancient castle. "King Henry stood on those parapets and watched his fleet fight the invading French in 1545."

"Aye, sir and he watched the *Mary Rose*, the pride of his fleet, roll over and sink." Kent swayed his head slowly from side to side. "Six hundred good English sailors died on her that day and she still lies on the muddy bottom." He surveyed the familiar landmarks around him. "Very near our present location, I am told."

Commander Beauchamp stood back and gazed up to the large billowing sails, filled with the land breeze. "Let us hope we fair better in this King's ship, Mr. Kent."

*****

Coal black eyes peered out from the puffy, red Irish face of Taber Lynch as he concentrated on the anchored ship below in the Fishbourne inlet. Lanterns hung from every available horizontal rigging line. The darkness was pushed back by the lantern light to reveal the ship's crew lifting canon from the ammunitions hoy tied along side. Small boats scurried like water beetles between the quay and the ship, carrying additional stores. He moved down the hillside towards the ship's stores stacked on the quay. Silently he watched as the chandler's men loaded the wide flat-bottomed dory with boxes and kegs of stores needed for the ship's long voyage. When he saw the dory was almost filled to capacity he glanced around making sure he was not noticed. He pulled the wide brim of his hat lower; shading his face, then picked up a box of galley wood and stepped onto the dory. The coxswain gave the signal to shove off as Taber joined the other men at the oars.

*****

Taber Lynch stepped onto the *Hawk's* main deck, looking around for a familiar face. A face he had an appointment with.

"You, there!" Bosun Braddock crossed the deck and grabbed Taber's arms. He snatched the man's arms up to read the markings on the box Taber carried. "Tis galley stores, ya have." He turned aft towards the hatch that led to the lower deck and galley. "Follow me, you lubber."

Taber glanced at the hurried activity around him then up to the quarterdeck. A Navy commander and lieutenant stood leaning over a chart spread atop the binnacle box.

"Hey you lubber!" Bosun Braddock grabbed Taber by the collar and pulled him towards the hatch. "I told ya ta follow me to the galley with them stores."

Taber's feet shuffled in the direction he was being pulled as he glanced back to the quarterdeck. His eyes locked onto the eyes of the commander who had looked down to see what the bosun was shouting at. They stared at each other for the briefest moment but to Taber it felt like the commander was looking into his soul.

Lieutenant La Rue stepped between Taber and the Commander's line of vision. "You do as ze Boson sez for you to do and stop ze skylarking."

"Something wrong, Captain?" Abe looked up from the chart and followed his captain's stare to the man with the box of firewood.

"Nothing, really." Nate bent back over the chart.

"Are you sure, sir?" Abe also bent over the chart but continued to watch Nate.

The Commander raised his head from the chart and stared as the bosun shoved the man toward the hatch. "That man seems familiar to me."

"There are lots of men about Portsmouth and the surrounding area right now, Sir." Abe lifted the dividers from beside the chart and traced their proposed route. "You very well may have seen him."

"I suppose you are correct, Mr. Kent." He watched the chart as Abe worked the dividers around the Isle of Wight and south toward the Caribbean.

Taber snapped his head back to the bosun who shoved him and his box of galley stores down the hatch; then Taber stepped away from the bottom of the ladder. He could see a light forward where men streamed down the forward hatch with boxes and sacks of galley stores like the one he carried. A one legged man and a young boy were placing stores on shelves. Light reflected off the shinny black paint of the newly installed twelve-pound canons. Sensing Bosun Braddock behind him, he sat the box of stores on the deck and turned to face the man who had abused him on the main deck. They both stared at each other in the dim light. Taber gave Braddock a wide grin. "Mathew Braddock, do ye have something for me?"

The bosun glanced forward to see if anyone had heard Taber call his name. The bosun pulled Taber aft into the darkness. "Taber Lynch, you'll get us both hanged if someone hears you call my name again."

"Sorry bosun, you have the right of that." Taber squeezed the bosun's arm to express his sincerity. "You have something for me then, Lad?"

"Aye, we sail on the next tide." He checked the activity in the galley. It was slowing with fewer deliveries as the loading of the *Hawk* neared completion. "We should be at the rendezvous in three weeks but in this cow it will more than likely be four."

"Do you have a chart for me, Bosun." Taber snapped as he realized that his time to leave the ship was nearing.

"Aye, Lynch but it be in me cabin. It will take but a minute to fetch." The boson scurried aft to the gunroom and his cabin.

Taber Lynch stared forward, watching the one legged cook and his mate place the last of the stores on shelves. He looked back to the gunroom, willing the bosun to hurry before he missed the last dory to carry him ashore. Darkness overtook Taber as the cook extinguished the last galley lantern. Hearing footsteps hurriedly approaching, he squeezed against the bulkhead, trying to make himself invisible in the darkness.

"Damn!" The bosun exclaimed as he neared the ladder and Taber. "Lynch!" The boson whispered into the darkness. "You still here?"

"Aye, Bosun, but I think you are too late for me to get off with the chandler's men." Taber's words carried the sound of desperation.

"Maybe so, Taber." Bosun Braddock started up the ladder to the main deck. "Let me check."

Taber held his body tensely against the bulkhead, almost as if he had become a part of the wood. Sweat oozed from under his wide brimmed hat and dripped from his brow into his eyes. The heat seemed to have intensified below deck since the one legged cook had closed the forward hatch. He blinked as the perspiration stung his eyes. Footsteps! Someone was descending the ladder. Taber attempted to squeeze himself closer to the bulkhead.

"No use, Taber!" it was the bosun. "The dories and the hoy have left the ship."

Taber Lynch let out his breath. "What do we do now, Braddock?"

The bosun raised his hand to strike Taber. "I told you not to call my name, you fool." The bosun caught the glint of Lynch's knife as the man held it to the bosun's midsection. He brought his hand down and reached under his warrant officer's jacket and retrieved the oil-skinned pouch, handing it to Taber. "Put the knife away and take this." He looked around the deck. "We will have to hide you until you can get over the side. Lynch tucked the oilskin pouch into the top of his trousers and followed the bosun.

*****

Commander Beauchamp stood forward and just to the right of the ship's wheel. First officer Kent was amidships at the quarterdeck's forward rail. Bosun Braddock stood aft of the men manning the capstan awaiting the order to retrieve the anchor. The tide was at its fullest and within minutes would turn to run out to sea again. Now was the time to weigh anchor and head to sea before the tide changed and pulled *Hawk's* stern seaward instead of landward as she now sat pointing towards the mouth of the inlet.

Commander Beauchamp nodded to the waiting first officer.

Mr. Kent yelled to the bosun. "WEIGH ANCHOR!"

"PULL AWAY, MEN." Bosun Braddock's thick Irish accent ordered the men to turn the capstan and lift the anchor.

Hawk edged forward until over the anchor. "Straight up and down, sir."

Nate stood with Major Scarlet, purposely looking seaward, allowing Abe Kent to take the *Hawk* to sea.

Mr. Kent smiled at his captain's back and the confidence it implied. "Lift away, Mr. Braddock." With the anchor off the bottom, the *Hawk* slowly drifted seaward. Mr. Kent looked up into the rigging, then back to the second lieutenant. "I'll have the top sails on her, if you please, Mr. La Rue."

Lieutenant La Rue shouted into the tops, "Man ze braces, make ze sail."

The sails handling was poor at best, plainly demonstrating the ship's crew was not accustomed to working together. Never-the-less, the sails filled with the land breeze and the ship moved towards the Solent. Nate spoke to Major Scarlet, "With sail handling like that no one will suspect us a navy ship." They watched the men in the tops tie off lines and put away the gaskets before descending to the main deck. "We will have to improve the sail handling considerably if we are to stop Black Caesar and his Irish benefactors."

"MAN OVERBOARD!" the shout came from the starboard bow.

Fourth Lieutenant Howard Foster ran to the gun deck and shouted to third lieutenant Levy. "We have a runner, Mr. Levy."

Sheldon Levy peered into the darkness, straining to see the swimmer. "Not likely on a ship of all volunteers, Mr. Foster."

Nate spoke from the quarterdeck. "I agree, Mr. Levy." He pointed to where the sound of the swimmer's splashes echoed back to the ship. "Major Scarlet, have your men see if they can shoot that man."

Major Scarlet motioned for the waiting Sergeant Thomas Christmas and two of his marines to fire on the swimmer. The two marine sharpshooters fired towards the sound of the swimmer's splashes but it was no use, the dark night hid the swimmer well. The sails billowed pushing the ship past the swimmer. Several minutes passed, as did the *Hawk* moving seaward, leaving the swimmer somewhere in the darkness of her wake.

Major Scarlet approached the captain. "I am sorry, sir, it is just too dark to make a good shot."

"You did your best, Major." Nate called to the first officer. "Mr. Kent, take a muster of all hands so we can find whom it is that does not enjoy our company." He gazed out into the night. "Take her West into the Solent, then south as we discussed, I will be in my cabin."

He turned to leave then stopped. "As soon as you have the muster complete inform me as to who the swimmer is."

*****

Abe Kent entered the captain's cabin and approached where Nate sat on the settee at the aft windows. For a moment they stared at the disappearing lights of the English shore. Nate broke the silence. "Well, Abe, do we know who the swimmer is?"

"I'm afraid not," Abe glanced down at the muster book in his hands, then held the book up for Nate to see the check marks by each man's name. "No one is missing, sir."

Nate paced to his desk, deep in thought. "Have Mr. Levy report as soon as he is relieved of his watch." He pulled the stuffed chair away from the desk, sat down then propped his feet on the desk while loosening his collar. "If we can find how Mr. Levy came to know our destination, perhaps it will shed some light on our swimmer.

Chapter Five

A Game for Men

Lieutenant Levy entered the captain's cabin with his foreword and aft hat in his hand. Nate glanced up to see a middle-aged man whose face carried a certain confidence as only a man of experience could. His face was round with a bushy mustache under a rather average looking nose, not too large and not too small. His hair was as black as Nate's own, except for a few streaks of gray, while his expression was that of a serious man with a purpose. His eyes scanned the cabin, no doubt similar to his cabin on the ship taken from him by the French privateer. "You send for me, sir?"

"Yes, lieutenant, come in," Nate studied the new style hat the lieutenant carried. It was so different than the traditional bicorn hat he and most naval officers wore. "Take a seat, Mr. Levy," he indicated the chair in front of his desk. "That is quite a hat you have there."

Levy glanced down to the new hat in his hand. "Yes, sir. The Portsmouth tailor told me it is the latest design permitted by the Admiralty."

"I see you wear your hair short, in the new fashion," Nate subconsciously reached back and stroked his queue, pulling the long hair downward. "Is it easier to maintain? Do you like it?" Nate's attempt to settle down the lieutenant with small talk did not appear to be working.

Levy sat stiffly in the chair, eyes ever roaming the cabin, searching for some unknown danger. "It does me just fine, sir." He answered with an irritated voice. "You asked me here to discuss my appearance, sir?"

Nate leaned forward, studying the man's eyes. *You can usually tell if a man is arrogant or merely nervous by the look of his eyes. No arrogance here, more like a man accustomed to asking the questions instead of being queried.* He answered Lieutenant Levy's question. "By no means, Mr. Levy, I did not." He reached to the front of the great white desk and retrieved an envelope. "However, I do find it interesting that a man of your sea experience has so readily taken to the modern dress." Commander Beauchamp gave Mr. Levy a slight smile.

Levy seemed to relax somewhat. "Well, sir," he ceased darting his eyes around the room and peered into his captain's face. "After I lost my ship to the Frenchmen I needed a change," his fingers, unknowingly, slipped through his short hair. "I obtained a position on the

Andromeda and began a new life in the Navy." Levy realized his fingers were raking his hair; he lowered his hand and rested it on the chair arm.

Commander Beauchamp nodded in understanding. Opening the envelope and withdrawing the papers. He placed succeeding papers aside until he came to the report from the captain of the *HMS Andromeda.* He quickly rescanned the contents of the page. "Captain Roebuck speaks well of you, Mr. Levy." Nate laid the paper down then ran his index finger down the page, rereading the lower paragraphs. "You have performed well and moved up the ranks in an unusually short period of time while assigned to the *Andromeda.*"

Levy stared to where Nate's finger lingered on the report. "I have worked hard to adjust to the Navy way of doing things, sir," Lifting his eyes he saw his new captain nodding in agreement. "I am more experienced than the younger officers and doing my duties properly came natural."

"Very good, Mr. Levy. I figured your experience as captain of your own vessel had served you well." Nate placed the report back in the envelope and returned it to the pile of papers. "May I offer you something to drink, Lieutenant?"

"No thank you, sir. I had a coffee just before coming off watch."

Both men stared at each other for a few short, silent seconds. Each man sizing the worth of the other.

Commander Beauchamp liked what he saw in this former merchant captain. He decided to use the direct approach to obtain the answer he sought. "Mr. Levy." He leaned forward slightly towards the officer. "Do you know where we are bound?"

Mr. Levy pulled his collar outward and ran his fingers around the edge; he released some imagined body heat and used the time to gather his thoughts before replying to the captain's query. "I have heard the *Hawk* is bound for the Caribbean, sir. That is why I volunteered when Mt. Kent asked for officers on the receiving ship."

Nate tapped his fingers lightly on the arm of his chair then asked, "Where did you hear this, Mr. Levy?"

"Sir, would it be proper to ask a question?" Levy shifted in the chair, more ill at east than nervous.

"Certainly, Lieutenant, by all means, ask away." Nate eased back in his chair to await Levy's question.

"Sir, could we pace?" Levy's round, mustached face turned a red hue.

Nate's eyebrows arched. "Pace? Mr. Levy."

"Yes, sir." Levy rose slightly from his seat, then slid to the edge of the chair. "I am accustomed to pacing while I am thinking."

Nate stood, sliding his chair back as he swung his hand toward the cabin's open deck space, which ran from the forward bulkhead and aft to the curtain covered cabin windows.

"Shall we, Mr. Levy, I too find pacing a comfort for thinking."

They quietly paced the cabin, side by side. Sheldon Levy, looking at the floor, gathering his thoughts. Nathan Beauchamp patiently waiting for Levy to speak. They paced the deck three times, forward then aft, then forward again. They reached the settee under the cabin's aft windows and began the turn to pace forward once more. Levy glanced over to Nate and began his story. "The *Andromeda* was sent into the yard for refitting. Some of the officers and men were assigned to other ships. I was assigned to the receiving ship." He looked closely into Commander Beauchamp's eyes to discern if the young officer was aware of how difficult it was for a Jewish officer to find a berth in the King's navy.

Nate nodded his head in understanding. "I am aware of the difficulties an officer of your faith faces to serve his King, Mr. Levy."

"Yes, sir, there are many." He slowed his pacing as he continued. "One evening I was taking a late dinner at a small inn not far from where the receiving ship's messenger boat is assigned on the quay." They reached the bulkhead and turned to pace aft. "While waiting for my dinner, I heard two men at the table behind me talking about a warship named *Hawk* being sent to the Caribbean for a special mission. One of the men told the other that he was having difficulties finding the kind of men they needed."

"Did they say anything else, Mr. Levy?" Nate queried.

"Well, sir, my dinner arrived and while I was talking to the serving girl the gentlemen departed before I realized they had gone." Levy stopped his pacing and lifted his arm towards the chair at the front of Nate's desk. "I've paced enough, sir."

"Yes, let us sit for a while." They both took their seats then Nate posed another question. "Could you recognize the men if you saw them?"

"Afraid not, sir," Levy looked at the floor, deep in thought. "They had accents."

"Did you know the accents, Mr. Levy?" Commander Beauchamp was seeking any way to identify the two men.

Mr. Levy's eyes darted up with a gleam of remembrance. "Aye, sir. I have been around Irishmen enough to recognize a thick Irish brogue when I hear one and I'd swear the other to be a Frenchman."

Nate stood to show Levy to the cabin door. "Thank you, Mr. Levy, you have been most helpful."

Levy stood, taking the captain's lead towards the door. "I hope I have truly been of assistance in what you seek, Captain Beauchamp."

"We seem to have a few mysteries, Mr. Levy, such as who spread the word of our mission and why a man who is not on the ship's roster runs as we weigh our anchor." Nate ushered the lieutenant through the door. "Time will tell,

Mr. Levy, in the mean time, we must keep a weather eye at all times. Who knows what lies ahead?" He extended his hand to the third officer. "At any rate I am certain we will put your experience to good use. Happy to have you with us, Mr. Levy."

Both the captain and the third officer snapped their heads forward to peer down the darkened passageway and the sound of shouting voices. The frantic voices increased in volume as they drew near. "Mr. Addington! Mr. Addington! You mustn't go aft!" Two screeching midshipmen rushed from the dimly lit passageway chasing a small furry brown creature. They skidded to a stop in front of the Captain just as the creature squeezed past Nate and ran into his cabin. "Oh, sir! I am so sorry. Mr. Addington escaped his cage." The taller of the midshipmen exclaimed through an out of breath red face.

"Whoa, gentlemen," Nate reached out and grabbed the taller midshipman's shoulders to keep the lad from careening into himself and Mr. Levy. "Who, or better yet, what is Mr. Addington?" he demanded.

The young midshipmen peered around the captain and third officer, into the great cabin. Nate and Mr. Levy followed the boy's eyes to see a small brown monkey calmly sitting atop Nate's great white desk.

"I'm waiting for your reply, Mr..." Nate realized he did not know the midshipmen's names.

"Edwards, sir, Midshipman Daniel Edwards." The lad turned slightly, nodding to his friend. "This is Midshipman Pierre Bouchard."

Nate turned and peered into the cabin to see the monkey lift his quill and gently tickled his face with the tip of the feather. Nate and Mr. Levy turned simultaneously to stare at the two red faced midshipmen.

Midshipman Edwards coughed, wiped his sweaty face, and drew a deep breath. "Sir, Mr. Addington is my pet." He gulped another breath and continued, "He was given to me by my father to keep me company on the long voyage." A nervous Edwards blinked his eyes and waited for the captain's reaction.

Captain Beauchamp cautiously stepped back into his cabin. "Mr. Addington? Why is he called Mr. Addington?" He glanced back at Mr. Edwards, his clear, green eyes demanding a reply.

Midshipman Edwards squeezed past Mr. Levy and stepped into the captain's cabin. His eyes darted about, taking in the elaborate decorations that adorned the captain's home at sea. He cleared his dry throat and rasped, "Father said the monkey had as much sense as Prime Minister Addington did when he made the peace with France."

"I am inclined to agree with your father on that particular point, however?"...Captain Beauchamp stopped mid-sentence and glanced to the squeaking pantry door to see Jasper peek into the cabin. Jasper saw the monkey and grinned. The four officers watched, in amazement as Jasper walked to the desk, reached his arms out. The monkey crawled up Jasper's arms and perched himself atop Jasper's shoulder.

A smile slid across Nate's face. "Mr. Edwards, if Mr. Addington is to be a member of *Hawk's* crew, I will expect him to be dressed like the rest of the seamen."

*****

While calling all hands to aft, per Captain Beauchamp's orders, Lieutenant Kent gazed around the ship while the hands awaited their captain to come to the quarterdeck. The deck was well lit from the many lanterns hung in the lower rigging. Now the time had come to inform the men of their destination and mission. Mr. Kent noticed the men gathered in small groups, Englishmen with Englishmen, Spanish with Spanish, Italians with Italians, all men grouped in the comfort of their fellow countrymen. The first officer did notice a group of Irish and Frenchmen had gathered together around the mainmast instead of with their respective national groups. He grinned when he saw Midshipmen Daniel Edwards and Pierre Bouchard nudging each other and laughing at some private joke. Mr. Addington pulled at his leash trying to reach some shiny object behind the boys. The young men had become fast friends and never seemed to be far from each other. Just behind the midshipmen stood the giant Moroccan, Akill Tocma. He had heard the midshipmen refer to the man as "Sinbad". The

Moroccan never seemed to be far from the two young men. *He seems to have adopted the lads.*

Mr. Kent walked to the aft rail and watched as the last twinkling lights from his beloved English soil blinked like dim stars, then disappeared as the *Hawk* drove that extra distance putting them just over the horizon and the last touch of England for what could be months or years. For several minutes his eyes remained fixed to where the lights had been, wondering if this voyage would be the one to give him that extra step to the next level in his naval career, a command of his own.

"Sir," Quartermaster Hall called the first officer from his thoughts. "The captain is on the quarterdeck."

Abe turned to the ever-smiling face of the quartermaster. He had heard the sailing master, Mr. McClain, say that Quartermaster Hall was a religious man who put God before all else. Others had said the man had once been a parson with his own church until some unknown occurrence caused him to take to the sea. At any rate Mr. Hall always saw the best in everything and his smiling face seemed to uplift those around him. "Thank you, Mr. Hall."

"Evening, Mr. Kent," Captain Beauchamp approached the ship's wheel, wearing a dark blue merchant captain's coat with a plain white shirt laced with a drawstring that opened at the neck. His trousers were light gray, and instead of his navy bi-corn hat, he wore a light green scarf pulled tightly around his head and neatly tied in the back. The scarf's long green tails whipped around his neck, pushed by the same winds that drove the *Hawk's* sails. A plain black tri-corn hat sat snugly atop the green scarf, pulled down low to fight the winds that attempted to blow it from the captain's head. He wore dull, black, thigh high Calvary boots. He ignored the watching seamen who mumbled to each other at the curious attire their captain now wore. Captain Beauchamp's eyes strained as they scanned up at the sails, watching as the last of the offshore wind filled the large, billowing sails, slowly pushing the old ship as best as could be expected. "Have you ordered for the chests to be brought on deck?"

"Evening, sir." Kent touched his hat. "Aye, sir, they should be coming on deck as we speak and as you can see, the men have been ordered aft."

Both officers stepped to the forward quarterdeck rail and looked down to the main deck. Mr. Levy moved about, barking orders, supervising a large group of idlers in laying huge chests in neat rows with three-foot passage between them. The groups of seamen mumbled, speculating in their own languages as to what the chests might contain and what the captain might tell them about their voyage.

When Mr. Levy's working party had all fifteen chests laid three abreast and aligned in five rows, he stood at the larboard side of the chests, looked aft to the quarterdeck and gave Captain Beauchamp a slight nod. Beauchamp nodded to Mr. La Rue who then moved from the quarterdeck to the main deck and stood abreast the chests opposite Mr. Levy.

The seamen moved about, viewing the rows of chests from different angles as if the new positions would reveal some secret about the chest, now displayed before them. Their mumblings began to rise above the wind and sea that slapped against the *Hawk's* hull.

"Men!" Captain Beauchamp shouted to draw the crew's attention. All hands stared aft to the quarterdeck and quietly, the *Hawk's* officers and men waited for the captain to continue. The sluice of waves burst against the hull as winds whipped across the deck and through the shrouds. The taunt lines and cords of the rigging hummed in the blowing wind. Some glanced up into the rigging as if the silence on deck allowed them to hear the humming for the first time. The moment had come to learn of their mission and the mystery of the chests between them and the quarterdeck. The captain continued. "Men, I know there have been many rumors as to our mission and our destination."

The *Hawk's* crew, officers and lower deck men alike, looked among themselves, nodding in concurrence. "Dat's a fo sure," mouthed the burley Italian sail maker, Alberto Trifiro. The men laughed, slapping each other on the back at the Italian's forwardness.

"Yes, I know I have heard of many myself," Beauchamp smiled. "From sailing to Africa to capture slavers, to the long voyage East to Batavia to fight oriental pirates."

The men nodded their heads acknowledging those rumors and more.

Beauchamp raised his arms to quiet the men once more. "Well men, part of it is correct."

The seamen stared at each other, wondering which parts of the rumors were true.

Nate placed his palms on the rail and leaned forward. "Lads, we are on a special mission for our King. Britain is in danger from spies and rebels." Standing erect he pointed forward of the starboard bow. The men turned and looked into the darkness where he pointed. "Beyond that horizon, Irish rebels who have been fairly treated by our King, are in league with vicious pirates to salvage gold and silver from a sunken Spanish treasure ship." He scowled as if in anger. "They intend to use that treasure to purchase weapons to do our country harm." He looked among the men, making eye contact with several. "Are we to allow that to happen?" he shouted to the watching men.

"NO!" came the unified reply.

Lieutenant La Rue grinned as the captain worked the men into a patriotic frenzy, foreigner and Briton alike. Lieutenant Levy looked about the proceeding curiously while Major Scarlet stared straight ahead from the quarterdeck as was expected of a proper marine.

"I know you are wondering what these chests are about." He swung his arm from larboard to starboard, above the chests.

"Aye!" They shouted in unison.

"A British ship cannot legally enter into Spanish waters," he nodded to La Rue and Levy who walked down the line of chest, flipping the lids open. The seamen leaned forward trying their best to see the contents of the chests. Mr. Addington pulled at his leash to see what he could see too. Beauchamp continued, "However." He glanced aft to petty officer Gaspar Salazar, nodded, and then watched as the British ensign was pulled down the halyard and the red and yellow Spanish flag took its place. Light from the captain's cabin flowed up through the skylight and illuminated the flag making it stand out in the surrounding darkness. He turned back to his audience of fired up seamen. "A Spanish merchantman can." Nate pointed to the now open chests. "These chests contain clothing not normally worn by King's men, but they will make our enemy believe we are what we appear to be." He turned and pointed to the Spanish flag flying high at the masthead. "From now until we meet the enemy, we are a Spanish merchant ship, a chameleon for our King."

The men cheered, "HUZZAH! HUZZAH! HUZZAH!"

Beauchamp felt the presence of Mr. Kent at his side; he reached over and took the edge of the black bundle Mr. Kent held. Pulling the black material as he moved, he stepped to the larboard four feet. Captain Beauchamp and First Officer Kent flipped the cloth up and over the rail. They pulled each side tight, allowing the bottom to drift down. The cheering men became silent and stared, opened mouthed, at the white skull and crossbones on the black field.

Nate stepped back slightly as Petty Officer Salazar relieved him from his position holding the black flag. He stood at the center of the flag and pointed down to the skull. "This is how we will catch our King's enemy." He glanced at the Spanish flag then down to the men as he continued, "We shall fly the Spanish flag to get into Spanish Florida, then when we sight the pirates and rebels, will fly this buccaneer banner." The silent men watched as their captain walked down the quarterdeck ladder and over to one of the starboard nine pound canon. "Then, gentlemen, they can accept us as brother pirates till we come close enough to board or we will use these long nines and the twelve pounders below on them."

The men cheered louder this time, "HUZZAH! HUZZAH! HUZZAH!"

"They won't expect a fat Spanish merchantman to have such sharp teeth, will they lads?"

Another round of cheers erupted from the men, "HUZZAH! HUZZAH! HUZZAH!"

"Now men, gather your new garb and pack away your own," he stepped back from the guns to clear a path for the anxious men

The men pushed and shoved to see who would have at the chests first.

Captain Beauchamp ran back up the starboard ladder, leaned over the rail, and shouted to the men, "Remember, lads, let's not be too navy like in the handling of the ship."

"That ain't gonna be no problem with this crew." Mr. McClain pointed out the obvious.

The men milled about the chest picking through the clothes, joking and nudging each other as they laughed at the captain's last remark.

Mr. Addington broke free from Mr. Edwards and sat in one of the chests, snatching brightly colored garments and throwing them among the chattering seamen.

Seaman Iodice, a smallish but hardy Italian from Naples held a hand full of mixed jewelry up to the quarterdeck. "Capitan! What about these earrings, sir? May we wear them?"

Nate grinned. "What else would pirates do with them, Mr. Iodice?"

The smiling Italian returned the captain's grin then turned to pass out the jewelry to the outstretched hand of his shipmates. Nate noticed Midshipmen Edwards and Bouchard reaching in among the seamen to get their share.

"Captain, I think that went rather well," Mr. Kent nodded his approval.

"Thank you, Mr. Kent, now it is time for you and the other officers to change out of those uniforms." Beauchamp pulled his coat lapel, shaking it at his officers. "The officers' clothing chests are in the gunroom, gentlemen."

Abe Kent stood watching the men dig through the chests. Some pulled a piece of clothing, held it up against themselves, shook their head then threw it down or swapped it with a messmate. He grinned and slowly shook his head at the spectacle. "What a game for men to play."

"What was that, Mr. Kent?" Nate queried.

"I was just thinking, sir." He nodded to the deck full of men rummaging through the clothing chests. "How many of us played pirate as children."

Captain Beauchamp ceased grinning. "Abe, we must play this game of pirate very well if we are to prevent the recovery of the gold and silver from the *San Pedro.*" Abe nodded his agreement and turned as he noticed Mr. La Rue and Mr. Levy approaching them. Nate turned to leave. "You have the quarterdeck, Mr. Levy." He motioned for the two remaining officers to follow him. "You, gentlemen, had best go below and choose your clothing before the other officers make off with choice pickings."

*****

The ship sailed on day after day, night after night, avoiding other ships and steering clear of land; she moved slowly on her secret journey south. Somewhere south of the Azores and north of the Madeira Islands she turned to the southwest toward the Caribbean Sea and the westward route to Spanish Florida. Three days later they hove too while stores were shifted aft to lighten her bow in hopes she would gain speed by slipping over the waves instead of ploughing through them. Two knots were added to her normal speed; enabling her to reach seven knots.

Confiding to Mr. Kent, Captain Beauchamp commented, "We certainly will not out run any ship this side of Holland."

*****

Mr. Kent ordered the mixing of the men of different nationalities in their watch standing sections and the crew's mess. Lieutenant La Rue divided the men into two watches, the larboard watch and the starboard watch. The larboard watch was made of the forward mess group that included Frenchmen and Irishmen, for the most part, with a few Spanish mixed in to fill the numbers required. The starboard watch was made of the remaining mixture of British and foreigners. Lieutenant La Rue was officer in charge of the larboard watch, while Lieutenant Levy took charge of the starboard watch.

Below decks, a large storage room divided the berthing areas; a narrow passageway connected the two. Lieutenant La Rue's larboard watch berthed in the forward compartment, while Lieutenant Levy's starboard watch berthed in the aft compartment.

In the starboard watch's aft berthing area, the mess tables, hanging from lines attached to the deck above, were now surrounded by a mixture of Spanish, Irish, British, Italian, and a few French seamen. The men learned of each other's backgrounds, experiences, skills and shortcomings. Friendships were made as well as enemies. For the better part, they had become a unified watch, working together for a single cause, the welfare of the *Hawk* and each other.

In the forward berthing area of the larboard watch the French and Irish sailors sat around the mess talking in small groups and waiting. They talked of home, things past and things to come. Most of the Irishmen had served together before. Bruce Flanagan sat on his chest, sharpening his knife on an old wet stone. Across from him sat old Gregory Campbell, sewing a patch on his shirt. Flanagan glanced up as Campbell yelped at sticking his finger with the sewing needle.

"Grego." Flanagan called to the older man.

"Aye, Bruce?" Gregory sucked the blood from the tip of his pricked finger.

Flanagan stopped the stroke of his knife against the sharpening stone and leaned toward his friend. "When will they come?"

"Ye must be patient." Campbell looked at the blood oozing from his finger then wiped it on his trousers. "Could be today or tomorrow or next week." He leaned over and studied the younger man's face. "Ye must be patient lad, they will come and we will defeat these British tyrants just like we did at Castle Bar in ninety-eight." He went back to sewing his shirt, looked up at his watching friend, and said, "You'll see, lad, you'll see."

*****

The officers spent the long hot days carrying out the normal ship's routine. Extra sail drill was conducted, as was gunnery practice. They came to know the seamen; which were the best top men and gunners along with every other task needed to run the ship efficiently. For the most part, they had become a well-practiced team, who worked cheerfully together despite their many ethnic differences.

The gun crews could fire off two rounds in two and one half minutes but, never the less, were constantly pushed towards better performance by the ship's master gunner, Mr. Folliot.

Normally the master gunner would remain in the magazine, supervising the measuring of cartridges for each round of shot. Marcel Folliot was not the normal British master gunner. Mr. Folliot had been a battery captain in the French Royal Artillery prior to the Revolution in his homeland. He had escaped to England after the Republicans began their cleansing of the Royalist with their new invention, the guillotine, and now he sought his revenge by serving the British King.

With the captain's encouragement Mr. Folliot now commanded the *Hawk's* batteries with Mr. Levy and his starboard watch, manning the lower twelve pounders, while Mr. La Rue and his larboard watch manned the main deck's nine pounders. Mr. Folliot threw all of his energy into seeking perfection in his gun crews. Resentful at first, the men grew to respect his knowledge and eagerness to teach.

They soon learned he would not ask of them anything he would not do himself. Competitions were held between the lower and upper batteries for which could load and run out the quickest, with the winning battery being rewarded, extra grog.

The gunner could often be heard shouting to his crews, "How do you expect to beat ze pirates when you fire ze guns like old wash-women?" These outbursts usually caused the men to grin and double their efforts. Afterwards the gunner would say "Perhaps you are, maybe as good as ze, how do you British say? Ah! Yes, ze lubber!" It was a little game he played with them, yelling and pushing them to be their best, then giving them a compliment small enough to let them know they had room to improve and then dismiss them for their earned ration of grog.

*****

Nate came up the ladder and stepped on to the main deck to the sound of Sergeant Major Christmas calling cadence as the marines marched forward to the mast. The sergeant major barked his order and the troop stopped. He barked again and the marines turned around, stamped their boots then came to attention. Nate heard snickering and chuckling. He turned and gazed around the deck. The seamen were doing their best to not laugh at the marines. Looking back at the marines, this time studying them to see what the seamen might find so humorous, then he saw it. The marines were dressed much as the seamen were, in their pirate attire, except they wore their white cross belts and shiny marine boots. Nate glanced around, looking for Major Scarlet. There he stood on the quarterdeck all five foot nine inches, 200 pounds of pure, by the book, British marine officer. His brown steady eyes were on the drill performance of his marines.

Nate climbed the ladder to the quarterdeck and motioned to attract the major's attention. "Might I have a word with you, Major Scarlet?"

The major did a left foot turn and marched over to the captain and snapped to attention as he rendered a salute. "Sir?"

Captain Beauchamp took the major's elbow and guided him to the aft rail and out of hearing range of the others on the quarterdeck. Nate smiled to keep from laughing as he counseled Major Scarlet. "Major, I can appreciate the marine traditions of drill and uniform usage, however, if we are to fool the enemy I am afraid the drill and wearing of marine boots and white cross belts will just not do."

Major Scarlet glanced over his shoulder. He could see his marines from the chest up, still at attention. Their white cross belts glowed in the morning sun. Turning back to the captain, his face blushed deep red. "I am sorry, Sir. I don't know what I was thinking." The major turned and called, "Sergeant Major Christmas!" The sergeant major answered, "Sir." Then ran towards the quarterdeck and his major.

Captain Beauchamp leaned towards the major and spoke lowly so only the major could hear. "Might I suggest you have the sergeant major dismiss the men to their quarters then have them remove the boots and cross belts?"

The major's eyes grew bright with understanding. "Very good, Sir." He stepped off to meet the oncoming sergeant major then stopped momentarily. "Thank you, Sir." He then continued to the sergeant major.

Mr. Levy stepped over to where Nate watched the major and sergeant major descend the quarterdeck ladder to the waiting marine squad. "If I may say so, sir. That was a decent thing to do."

Nate glanced at the third officer. "I don't know what you mean, Mr. Levy." Then he moved to the ship's wheel and glanced down to the compass in the binnacle box.

"Just the same, sir." Levy followed the captain. "It would have been embarrassing for the major to have the marines strip their belts and boots on deck for all to see his error."

The captain looked up as Levy approached. "Seemed like the right way to handle things, Mr. Levy."

"Aye, sir, it was." Shell Levy looked up to the sails. "A good lesson for us all."

Chapter Six

The Mutiny

Somewhere two hundred miles due west of the Cape Verde Islands, the *Hawk* obtained the trade winds and Beauchamp placed her on a course for the northern end of the Leeward Islands.

Captain Beauchamp relied on the teachings he learned while serving with Captain Horatio Nelson. Captain Nelson surmised it to be healthier for his seamen to be issued two hammocks each so that one is washed and dried while the other is in use. This assured the men always had a clean, dry sleeping area. Nate ordered the reluctant purser to issue the same for the *Hawk's* men.

After so many days at sea and the heat of the tropics the ship's purser, Evan Pearce, reported that water was turning foul, green in color and brackish to the taste. Meat in the casks, as on all His Majesty's navy ships, had been in the casks for years, some packed and salted during the last war, and now had begun to turn. Ship's biscuit had to be tapped on the mess tables to loosen the weevils, which had infested the bread.

Like the food and water the men too began to turn. Free time between sail handling and gun drill in the beginning seemed all too short now because of inactivity and restlessness to be ashore, off duty time became much too long. Arguments and fights broke out between the men of the lower decks. Captain Beauchamp noticed that the officers had also become short with each other. Nate realized he lacked the tools he needed to keep the men occupied and too fatigued to argue and fight among themselves. The men needed to be kept busy, as were the men on regular navy ships. Ships that required scrubbed decks, fresh paint, smart rigging and shiny brass.

Nate snapped his head forward at the screeching of foreign and English babbling. He rushed to the forward quarterdeck rail and looked to the main deck. Seamen circled around to watch. Quartermaster Hall and Italian seaman Iodice were red faced and shouting at each other.

Hall lunged forward; hands outstretched reaching for the Italian's throat. "You bloody Papist, I'll squeeze yer gizzard till yer eyes pop out."

Although small in stature the Italian was wiry and strong from years of hard work at sea. He danced back as the quartermaster lunged. Hall stumbled on the hatch combing and fell to his knees. Using the agility developed over years of climbing through ships rigging, Iodice stopped his backward motion and in one swift movement rushed forward, grabbed Hall's hair pulling his head back, at the same time he reached into his belt and retrieved his knife and raised his hand to slice Hall's throat.

A strong hand grabbed the Italian's arm. "No, no, Michael, that is not the way." Iodice turned to see his friend, Luigi looking down at him. "This is nothing to kill a man for." Michael Iodice lowered his hand and released Quartermaster Hall's hair. Sweat ran down Hall's flushed face, he pushed his hair back into place and struggled to stand. Luigi continued speaking softly to his friend, calming down his Italian temper. "People are different, you must remember, not everyone believes as we do." Luigi took Iodice's knife and placed it back in his belt. "Our way is not the way of others." He nudged his friend toward the kneeling quartermaster. "Help Mr. Hall to his feet and apologize." Michael Iodice reached his hand to the quartermaster. "I am'a so sorry signori." Hall took the offered hand and Iodice pulled the big man to his feet. "I mean a you would a go to a hell if'a you was de Italian and divorce'a you wife."

The big man straightened his clothes and grinned at the smaller Italian. "Well, why did ye not say so in the first place, lad?" He reached over and placed his arm around seaman Iodice and walked him back to where they sat talking before the misunderstanding. "Have ye any wheel handl'n experience?" Hall patted seaman Iodice's back. "Have ye any intensions o stay'n in the navy, lad?"

Luigi Colavecchio shook his head at the two men walking away. He returned to the barrel he sat on earlier, picked up his book, parchment and quill then continued his studies.

Captain Beauchamp squinted his eyes to read the title of the book in the tall Italian's hands, *The Science of Mathematics.* Seeing the disagreement resolved, he eased away from the rail before he was seen and forced to take action against the two men.

Nate was disturbed about the edginess among the crew. He glanced down to the tall Italian and a different train of thought crossed his mind. He looked around the quarterdeck and notice Midshipmen Daniel Edwards and Pierre Bouchard at the larboard rail watching seagulls dive for fish. "Mr. Edwards, a moment, if you please."

Edwards abandoned his friend and reported to the captain. "Sir?"

Nate nodded to the main deck and the tall Italian. "Tell me about that fellow."

Edwards followed the captain's stare. "Oh, that is Luigi, sir."

Nate stared at the midshipman and arched his eyebrows. "Mr. Edwards, please continue."

Edwards looked in the captain's inquiring eyes then back to the man seated on the barrel. "He is just a simple seaman, sir."

Captain Beauchamp nodded toward Luigi. "A simple seaman, I think not, he has an air about him of an educated man and what he reads is certainly not the choice of any simple seaman I have known, that is if most seamen could read."

"I suppose not, sir." Edwards concurred as the captain moved them both away from the rail.

"See what you can find out about him and report back to me as soon as possible." Nate ushered the lad on his way and continued to pace the quarterdeck deep in thought on how to occupy the men in their off duty hours.

A loud crash came from the forward part of the ship. All the hands on deck, not on duty, rushed to the forecastle to investigate. Nate stopped Midshipman Bouchard from following the men rushing forward. "Mr. Bouchard!"

The midshipman stopped just short of the quarterdeck ladder. "Sir?"

Nate nudged the lad aside as he descended the ladder. "You have the quarterdeck."

Bouchard lowered his head at the disappointment of missing the ruckus then realized he had been given command of the ship, be it temporary. "Aye, aye, sir." He smiled, placing his hands behind his back, and commenced pacing the deck as the captain had just been doing.

Captain Beauchamp reached the forecastle to see the crew gathered around two men wrestling on the deck. Each man was cheering for his messmate. He pulled men aside and others stepped back when they recognized who pushed through them. When he reached the center he saw the American Mantell and the Irishman Flanagan locked together, rolling around the deck. It seemed that Flanagan was getting the better of the fight, having penned Mantell's head between a cleat and the bulwark. Bosun Braddock and two of his mates held several of Mantell's messmates from stopping the fight.

"Mr. Braddock! You will stop that fight this instant!" Nate shouted over the crowd noise.

"Aye, sir." Braddock knuckled his forehead and moved to break up the fight. Mantell's messmates, who were rushing to separate the two seamen, passed him. When Braddock reached the two fighters they had been pulled to their feet. He grabbed Mantell's collar. "You are noth'n but a trouble make'n sod." He snatched the seaman forward. "I'll see you flogged for this."

"Belay that, Mr. Braddock!" Nate stepped between Bosun Braddock and Topman Mantell.

Bosun Braddock pulled Mantell's collar forward with Mantell lunging with it. "But Captain, this swab be a troublemaker," Braddock yelled.

"Mr. Braddock, you forget your place!" Nate angrily snatched Braddock's hand from the topman's collar.

"Beg pard'n, sir, I ment no harm." Braddock's fictitious grin irritated the Captain. "I were jus do'n my duty, sir."

"I'll take over here bosun." Nate glanced around at the watching seamen. "Break it up, you men go about your business." He turned back to Mantell and Flanagan. "You two get back to your messes and calm down and clean up." The two men knuckled their foreheads then Mantell went aft to his mess while Flanagan moved forward to the ladder leading to the forward mess.

Nate began walking back towards the quarterdeck when an idea came to him. He raced down to his cabin stopping only briefly to have the marine outside his door pass the word for all officers, not on duty, to lay aft to his cabin.

When Lieutenant Foster was the last to arrive, Nate asked him to close the door. He glanced around the cabin at the attire of his officers. *They do look like a bunch of pirates.* He gave a slight grin and commenced addressing his officers. "Gentlemen, our water is growing foul, our food is turning that way and the men are at each other's throats." He scanned the cabin full of the ship's officers. Here and there gold earrings dangled from the nodding heads. "Mr. Levy, yesterday there were three fights in the starboard watch," he turned back to his desk, shoved the papers toward the back as he cleared a space to sit, then turned to the officers. "To what do you attribute that to, sir?"

Levy cleared his throat as he stood. "The foul food and water that you mentioned and too much idleness, sir." He glanced back to be sure of the location of his seat as he sat back down.

Nate sat on the edge of the desk. "Right you are, Mr. Levy. They are too long from home. They are missing their activities ashore and their loved ones and they are faced with way too much time to think about them." He studied the implements on his desk, gathering his next words. "The *Hawk* is like no other navy ship, and we cannot occupy them with normal navy duties such as shining brass and scrubbing decks, that would defeat our ruse." Nate rose from the corner of the desk and paced to the cabin's aft windows, rubbing his chin in thought, then, he returned to the seated officers. "I was thinking we might hold a competition for the men,"

Lieutenant La Rue stood to be heard. "Monsieur Captain, I would like to point out that my watch has had very few fights and seem to get along just fine."

Master McClain raised his hand and spoke up. "What kind of competition did you have in mind, Captain?"

Nate nodded to the ship's master, acknowledging his query, then turned to address the second lieutenant. "Mr. La Rue that may be true about the larboard watch, however, we will need the larboard and starboard watches to compete against each other." He turned to the ship's master. "Mr. McClain, I had a seaman's contest in mind, one where the two watches would have representatives train and compete in everyday tasks which make our seamen unique."

Surgeon Badeau raised his hand. Upon recognizing the Frenchman, Nate thought of the background of the smallish, dark haired man with the grim forbearance. Once a doctor with a prosperous practice in Marseille, his world collapsed when his royalist support caused the Republican government to place a price on his head. He now served the Royal navy as one of the few true medical men serving as a ship's surgeon. The *Hawk* was fortunate to have such a man tend the men and officers. He acknowledged the doctor. "Yes, Mr. Badeau?"

"Please excuse a medical man's lack of knowledge, Monsieur Captain, but what kind of task have you in mind?"

"Not a bad question, doctor." Nate sat on the desk again. "I was thinking along the lines of perhaps races up the rigging, marlinspike, knot tying, ivory carving, anything to keep the men busy and out of mischief."

"Captain," Major Scarlet irritably shifted his sea officer's coat, an indication of his distaste for every form of attire with the exception of his marine major's uniform. "How will one day's competition keep the men at ease?"

"From now on, we will encourage the men to practice during their off duty hours." He looked around the cabin to see the officers were questioningly, staring back at him. "That ought to reduce the tension below deck I shouldn't wonder."

The officers and warrants nodded and mumbled their agreement. "Good. Mr. La Rue and Mr. Levy, I will expect you gentlemen to meet and decide on what tasks will be included in the competition and an event date as well to encourage every man in your watch section to practice and participate."

The Greek master carpenter, Andreas Pappas, timidly raised his hand to speak.

Nate nodded to the carpenter. “You have a question, Mr. Pappas?”

Poppas stood rolling his hat around in his clenched hands. “What a will a da prize a be for a da winners?” He sat down then quickly stood again with a sheepish grinned. “Ah, sir?” Grinning and glancing around the cabin, he nodded to the other officers and warrants as he sat back down.

“Well, that is a question well put, Mr. Poppas,” Nate stroked his chin and wrinkled his brow as if pondering the answer to a tactical battle question. “I think the officers could donate a little from each of our shares of the prize money we will receive when we take the pirates and rebels; say enough to provide the event winners with an extra share apiece.”

La Rue spoke up. “Let us hope there is prizes money to share, Monsieur Captain.”

Captain Beauchamp strode over to the cabin’s outer bulkhead and stroked the wood. “She is slow and cumbersome, I’ll grant you that, Mr. La Rue. However, we must have faith in our Trojan Horse.”

*****

The following days found off duty seamen throughout the decks and rigging practicing their seamen skill. Men of the starboard watch were much more noticeable than the men of the larboard watch. While the starboard watch hands vigorously went about their preparation for the competition in large numbers of excited seamen; Lieutenant La Rue's larboard watch seemed to be going through the motions in small numbers. Never the less, for the most part, the men were kept busy and the discontent subsided over the succeeding days and weeks.

*****

With a bright sunny sky and a smooth running sea the *Hawk* departed the westward currents of the great Atlantic Ocean and made her turn to enter the Eastern fringe of the Caribbean Sea. Instead of entering the well-used Anegada Passage at the northern end of the Leeward Islands, Captain Beauchamp chose the less crowded northern route, through the Virgin Islands. With luck, the *Hawk* would be north of Puerto Rico in three or four days, sailing past Cuba before the end of the week, and on to the Florida Keys shortly thereafter. The *Hawk* would be approaching Spanish Florida in no more than two weeks time.

Nate Beauchamp came up the quarterdeck ladder and stood watching Mr. Kent at the aft rail. Kent leaned on the rail scanning the horizon with a glass. "Mr. Kent," Nate spoke to the first officer as he joined him.

Kent passed the glass to Nate. "She still follows us, sir."

Nate placed the telescope to his eye and followed the direction of Kent's outstretched arm.

"She looks fairly small." He adjusted the glass into focus. "Most likely a commerce raider or privateer." He closed the glass and glanced aloft to see how the sails drew the wind, then glanced aft to the see the glair of the sun's reflection on the sea almost hide the ship on the horizon. "With the traffic in these waters she might even be one of our own."

Kent shaded his eyes with the palm of his hand, squinting to see the ship. The mystery ship had slid behind the horizon and out of sight. "I'll keep a good lookout aloft just in case she is not a friend."

"Very well, Mr. Kent." Nate walked towards the bow to study the islands now lying off to the starboard bow. He stepped down the ladder onto the main deck and traveled a few feet before the *Hawk* rolled to starboard forcing him to grab a shroud to steady himself. The ocean kicked up a bit as the waters rushed through the beginning of the Anegada Passage. Rollers are what his father had called them. He smiled at the remembrance of his now deceased father.

He steadied himself and got his feet under him before moving on forward towards the bow. Men sat about the deck doing the usual things off duty men do to beat the monotony of Sunday at sea. Practice for the competition was not held on Sunday, as it was a make and mend day as well as a day of rest for those not on duties. A few sat in groups chatting, no doubt about some ship they had served or some far off port they might have visited in the past or even about loved ones at home. It did not matter to Nate, he was happy to see them getting along better these last few weeks.

Forward of the ship's main hatch, members of Lieutenant La Rue's larboard watch sat in small groups of twos and threes, talking low, a few were drawing their knives across wet stones, then holding the blades edge up for a messmate to witness the skill required to hone the blade to such sharpness. Nate nodded to an older Irishman sitting on an upturned bucket. The old man removed his long stem pipe, smiled and knuckled a salute as the captain passed on his way forward.

As he began to climb the foredeck ladder he thought how much the old ship looked like the relic she was. Few modern ships had raised forward and aft decks any more.

He reached the foredeck to find Jasper, the two midshipmen and their Sinbad, the Moroccan, Mr. Tocma. He wondered what would make a man of the desert seek employment on the sea, then doubted the answer would ever be revealed.

Nate stepped closer to see what the men and boys were about. Midshipman Edwards sat on a shipping crate with no shirt. Instead a cloth was draped around his shoulders. Jasper stood to the midshipman's side. He held a cork behind the young man's left ear while Sinbad stood in front of the boy with a small sail needle. Midshipman Bouchard stood to the side holding a fidgety Mr. Addington while he nervously watched the proceedings. He too, wore no shirt but had himself wrapped in a piece of old sailcloth. They were too busy to notice the captain as he observed them. Sinbad and his sail needle drew near the boy's ear. Jasper pulled Edward's ear away from his head and pushed the cork tightly behind. Sinbad talked softly and smiled at the lad then raised his left hand and struck Edward's ear with a flat piece of wood then jammed the sail needle through the ear into the cork. Edwards jumped and screeched out in pain. Mr. Addington also screeched and tried to pull free from Bouchard to get to his master. A tear trickled down his cheek. Jasper rubbed the boy's arm. "Now. Dat don't hurt yo none, do it, Mista Edwards?"

"It most certainly does hurt," the lad ran his fingers around the new hole in his ear and the sail needle stuck into the cork.

Jasper leaned in front of the boy's face. "Yo wants ta look like a pirate, don'ts ya?" He turned his head to show the lad his shiny hoop earring running through his newly swollen ear lobe.

"I...I guess I do." Young Edwards stammered.

Jasper motioned to the Moroccan who stepped forward with a shiny gold hoop earring held up for the lad to see. "Ain't dat purdy, Mista Edwards?" Jasper nodded and Sinbad dangled the gold earring in the lad's face. While Edwards focused his attention on the earring, Jasper took hold of the cork and sail needle and yanked them apart. Edwards flinched and Sinbad quickly slid the earring through the hole and snapped the back. "Now dat weren't so bad, was it Mista Edwards?" Jasper smiled at the shocked midshipman.

Edwards returned Jasper's smile through teared eyes. "No, Jasper it hardly hurt at all."

"Good!" Jasper stood up smiling at Mr. Bouchard.

Bouchard began to ease toward the ladder to the main deck. Jasper nodded to Sinbad and Mr. Edwards. They laughed; nodding to each other then lunged and caught Bouchard just as he was starting to run. Mr. Addington clung to his back, fearfully digging his claws into Bouchard's flesh. The three pursuers drug him back kicking and screaming. The noise brought the off watch hands up the ladder to see what the commotion was about. When Midshipman Bouchard saw the men watching he bravely sat on the crate and awaited his turn to be pierced for his new earring.

Nate enjoyed the spectacle then moved on to the bow and left them to their fun. His knee pressed against the starboard rail to steady him against the rollers. He pulled the glass from where it was tucked into his belt, and scanned the starboard horizon. *Hawk's* bow un-expectedly rose, pushed up by a larger than normal wave. This area was known to have the occasional rogue wave. If this was a rouge wave it was in its infancy. Never the less, it jostled Nate from his place against the bow bulwark. He reached out and grabbed the root of the bowsprit to steady himself. Regaining his composure he glanced aft to see if anyone had noticed his awkwardness. No one was looking in his direction and he grinned at the thought that he had almost lost his composure and spilled on the deck like a lubber. Nate brought the glass up to his eye again and scanned the islands to starboard, looking for the entrance to the Sir Francis Drake Channel. He need not have worried, before him was a wide channel running north of Virgin Gorda. Glancing to a noise behind him he saw Topman Bobby Mantell coiling a loose line on the foredeck. "Mr. Mantell, be so kind as to inform the second officer to turn the ship to run north of that island to starboard."

Topman Mantell knuckled his forehead and turned to report to Mr. La Rue. "Aye, aye, sir."

"Mr. Mantell, also inform Mr. La Rue I will be aft shortly, if you please."

*****

The *Hawk* healed over as she made her starboard turn towards Virgin Gorda and Sir Francis Drake Channel. The turn was sharper than was the norm. Nate felt the difference and glanced aft to see that even at her slow top speed of seven knots, the much too sharp turn caused seawater to splash above the bulwark. She dug her nose deeply into the large swells flowing down the channel and shook as the lines and sails vibrated from a contrary wind now blowing across her quarter. He rushed aft to give orders to ease the turn and keep the top-heavy ship from rolling over on her side, then saw the deck and rigging covered with men from both watches pulling lines and adjusting sail. First Officer Kent had rushed up from the gunroom to take command from Lieutenant La Rue and along with Master McClain was directing the trimming of the sail and the easing of the helm. *Hawk* leveled somewhat, as the trimmed sail pushed her steadily toward the channel.

All heads snapped upward as a scream descended from the main topgallant yard. A man crashed to the deck and laid crushed in a pool of his own blood. Nate rushed to the downed man to find Doctor Badeau bending over the body. He waited for the doctor's diagnosis. Doctor Badeau stood shaking his head. "Dead, Monsieur Capitan." He looked back down to the body. "From the moment he crashed to ze deck," The doctor faced the captain. "Every bone in 'es legs are broken. His pelvic is shoved upward into his spine."

A head came pushing through the gathered officers and men. "It were that damned Mic, Flanagan," Mantell turned to face Captain Beauchamp. "I saw him push Sam Miller from the yard."

"That ain't so, Bobby Mantell." Bosun pulled free of the crowded men and stepped over Miller's body. "Bruce Flanagan were below with me, inventorying in the rope and line locker."

"That's a lie, Bosun Braddock. I was on the fore topgallant look'n aft when Flanagan shoved old Miller off his perch." Bobby pointed at the main topgallant and stood looking up with an open mouth. Following his gaze all the officers and men looked up to an empty topgallant.

"You better be sure, Mantell afore ye accuses a man." Braddock grinned at Mantell as he looked about the gathered men as if in search of Bruce Flanagan. "I left Flanagan ta finish the inventory, so ya see, perhaps yer eyes played tricks on ye."

Mantell mumbled as the men began to drift away. "Wer't no trick I saw, Mathew Braddock."

"Thank you, doctor." Nate nodded to the body on the deck. "Mr. Levy, please see to preparing Mr. Miller for burial and commence an investigation into the incident."

When Nate reached the quarterdeck, Mr. Kent had taken Lieutenant La Rue aft for a dressing down. "Lieutenant La Rue, that ship handling was below what I would expect of a midshipman." Kent's blond hair whipped about his blood flushed face; still he calmly controlled his anger. "What were you about, sir?" He paced to and fro in front of the second officer, quelling his temper. "Any midshipman and tar alike would know a ship of this type can not make such a close wind turn." Kent stopped poking his nose inches from the red faced Frenchman. "Well, sir? I am waiting for your explanation."

"Monsieur Kent, it was not my fault, I did not order ze quartermaster to turn ze ship so close to ze wind." La Rue loudly pleaded his case.

Quartermaster Hall released the wheel to his mate and rapidly stepped across the deck toward the second lieutenant, fist clenched with gritted teeth. "You lie'n frog."

Nate grabbed the passing quartermaster's arm, pulling Mr. Hall to his side. "I'll not have my officers arguing on the quarterdeck like common merchants haggling in a market place." He nudged the quartermaster toward the ladder to the main deck. "You both will spend the remainder of the watch in your quarters." He waited for Mr. Hall's head to disappear down the ladder then he motioned for the second officer to follow. "We will discuss this tomorrow, when you both calm down and have clear heads."

Abe Kent came to stand next to Nate. "One would think that man intentionally intended to wreck the *Hawk*." Nate glanced at Abe questionably then both watched La Rue descend the quarterdeck starboard ladder. As he briskly crossed the deck to the ladder leading to the gunroom, Bosun Braddock stood up from his messmates and made a move toward the second lieutenant. La Rue shook his head and descended the gunroom ladder. Braddock briefly glanced up to the watching captain and first officer, then back to the where La Rue had just disappeared. The scowl on his face, accentuated by his wrinkled brow and pouting lips, openly displayed his displeasure of his watch officer's treatment by the captain and first officer.

Abe Kent spoke first, “That Irishman seems to be very fond of his French officer.” Nate nodded. “He does, indeed.” He looked up to see the sails drawing well and the ship now under control. “Strange bedfellows, I should think.”

*****

Commander Nathan Allen Beauchamp, captain of His Majesty’s Ship *Hawk,* sat at the great white desk, deep into his daydream of the lovely Irish woman with the flaming red hair and luscious red lips. They were dancing closely at a great ball. He was the guest of honor after defeating a French ship of the line with his antiquated *Hawk.* Dukes, admirals and the King applauded the lovely couple as they whirled around the dance floor.

“Sir!” The marine sentry called and patiently waited a moment to be recognized by the captain. “I called, sir, but there was no answer, so I thought something might be amiss.”

Nate awoke from his daydream and sat staring at the waiting marine. “I am sorry, corporal. I was occupied in thought.” He rustled the papers in front of him, picking up the top one and pretended to read it. “What is it you require, Corporal Anderson?”

He watched the large bull of a corporal nervously begin his announcement again. “Sir, the Italian seaman, Colavecchio, has reported as ordered.”

Nate laid the paper aside. “Pass him in if you please, corporal.”

Luigi Colavecchio entered the captain's cabin with a curled up red dyed canvas cap in his hands. "You send for me, sir?"

"Please have a seat, Mr. Colavecchio." Nate glanced to the sounds of Jasper moving around in the pantry just off the main cabin. "I understand you have been a teacher of some sort, Mr. Colavecchio." It was a statement rather than a question.

The tall Italian eased back in the chair, at ease in the presence of the captain. "Yes, sir. I taught English in Naples and Italian in London." He laid the red hat on the arm of the chair. "Mathematics is my subject of choice."

"Very good, Mr. Colavecchio. I have need of such talents." Nate pulled the muster book from under a canvas dispatch bag. "I am in need of a clerk, of course, it would require you relinquish your position forward and move aft with the warrant officers."

A surprised Colavecchio leaned forward slightly. "It would please me, sir, to be able to apply my preferred traditional profession instead of my newly acquired seamen skills."

The captain picked up his quill, dipped it in the ink well then pulled the muster book toward him. "There are collateral duties, I'm afraid."

The tall Italian suspiciously slid farther back in the chair and waited for the preverbal shoe to drop. "What might that be, Captain?" He watched the captain's hand move over the muster book, knowing it listed all the crew and each man's assigned job on the ship.

The dipped quill hovered above the white pages of the *Hawk's* muster book. "We have two midshipmen aboard and no one to attend their lessons." He studied the Italian's reactions as he spoke. "The master attends to their navigational studies but they are in dire need of attention to mathematics and trigonometry among other things."

Colavecchio grinned. "I think I am capable of that particular collateral duty, sir."

Jasper poked his nose just past the pantry door and cleared his throat.

Nate glanced to the door. Jasper smiled and nodded toward the soon to be captain's clerk. "Ah, yes, do you think you might be able to teach this unworthy colonial as well, Mr. Colavecchio?"

The new clerk glanced up at Jasper then back to the captain. "I think he may benefit from some instruction, sir."

"Good, Mr. Colavecchio." Nate entered the change of assignment in the muster book. "You can report back here as soon as you move your gear aft." He looked at the stack of paperwork scattered over the great desk. "Then perhaps we can find the bottom of this mess."

The newly appointed clerk passed through the captain's door, with a slight grin on his face, and then headed forward to fetch his dunnage.

Nate sprinkled sand over the muster book to dry the newly inked entry.

"Sir!" Corporal Anderson stood holding the cabin door open to announce another visitor.

Nate rolled his eyes upward acknowledging Anderson. "Sir, the purser wishes a word with the captain."

Captain Beauchamp motioned for the corporal to pass the purser into the cabin. "Yes, Mr. Pearce. You wish to see me?"

"Aye, sir. I have just come from inspecting the stores in the forward hold." Nate nodded and the purser continued. "Sir, all the water in the forward hold is foul."

The captain nodded. "Yes, I suspected as much; too long in the cask."

"No, sir, not too long in the cask." Pearce glanced left then right as he leaned over the desk. He lowered his voice to assure only the captain might hear his next words. "Seawater, sir."

Nate sprang to his feet. "Seawater? Are you positive, Mr. Pearce?"

"Aye, sir. I just checked the casks day before last and it were tainted from being in the cast so long but it were not contaminated with seawater."

"Have you inspected the water casks in the aft stores hold?" Nate queried.

"Aye, sir, that I have, and the water is green, but drinkable."

"Repeat this to no one, Mr. Pearce, we may have a traitor among us trying to sabotage our mission and if word gets out we will not be able to set a trap for him." Nate paced the cabin then abruptly turned to the purser and thought aloud. "Mr. Kent is on watch." He stroked his chin in thought. "Mr. Pearce, fetch Mr. Levy and return with him as soon as you can."

The small beady-eyed man turned and hurriedly exited the cabin while the captain contemplated the fouled water.

*****

Pearce and Mr. Levy slipped into his cabin like thieves in the night. If the problem at hand were not so serious, Nate would have smiled at their sense of secrecy. He waved them aft to the settee under the cabin's aft windows. "Gentlemen, thank you for coming so soon." He offered the two officers a seat as he slid over to accommodate them. He addressed Lieutenant Levy first. "Has Mr. Pearce informed you of our fouled water, Mr. Levy?"

"Aye, sir, he has." Shell Levy replied.

"Do you have any suspicions, Mr. Levy?"

"Sir, I just cannot trust having Frenchmen aboard, and that La Rue is a shifty character." Levy sat perched on the edge of the settee. "Those Irishmen in his watch section are just as shifty, always keeping to themselves and talk in whispers whenever anyone else is around." He angrily stood and took a step to pace, realized where he was and returned to his seat. "I think it best to place a guard on the aft stores hold to protect the water there."

Nate rose from the settee and walked to his desk, then back. "I think not Mr. Levy." The surprise in Levy's eyes showed a questioning of the captain's judgment. Nate continued.

"Should we place guards on the water, the person or persons we seek will know we are on to them." He shook his head. "No, I think we need to set a trap."

Shell Levy's interest perked up. "Aye, sir, that is what we need to capture these traitors."

"Mr. Pearce, go about your duties as if nothing has occurred." The captain sat back on the settee. "And, Mr. Levy, you choose a few men that we can trust to hide among the water cask to catch the culprit, should he try to do damage to our remaining water supply." He stood once more as he continued. "Enough men to capture the culprits in case there are more than one." He escorted the two officers to the cabin door. "Best have them stand shifts; we will need them alert at all times."

*****

Midshipmen Pierre Bouchard and Daniel Edwards sat scrunched behind two great water casks in the hot and dark aft stores hold. To the right and left of the young men were eight of the most trusted men of the starboard watch. Sinbad sat closest to the lads. They patiently waited for the traitor to show himself but three hours into their watch no one came. The two boys had long ago given up their restlessness and now lay against the hull behind the water barrels.

"Daniel." Pierre nudged his friend.

"Sssssshhh!" Daniel admonished Pierre for his loud breaking of the silence. He whispered low. "Do you want to give us away?"

"No one is coming, Daniel." Pierre strained his eyes to see Daniel's face.

"Why would you say such a thing, Pierre?"

"Because I heard Nolan and Flanagan talking last night." Pierre leaned forward, trying to see Daniel's face in the pitch darkness.

"They know we have set a trap for them?" Daniel abruptly sat up.

"No, Daniel, they were talking about taking over the *Hawk*." Pierre looked around, straining to see if any of the men had heard him.

Daniel chuckled. "Oh, Pierre, how can two men hope to overtake the ship?"

Pierre excitedly raised his voice. "Not just those two, the whole of La Rue's larboard watch."

Daniel Edwards leaped to his feet. "Why did you not speak of this before?" he rushed for the aft door. "We must tell Captain Beauchamp."

He reached the door with Pierre and the seamen close behind. Daniel pulled on the door opening it slightly, then it was snatched from his hand and slammed closed. "What the...?" They heard the bar slam down on the other side of the door, locking them in the hold. He turned to stare into the darkness of the hold. "We must find a way out of here."

*****

The *Hawk* slowly edged westward, to the south lay Mosquito Island. The yellow sun sent streaks of bright light down the deck. The larboard watch had just assumed the deck as members of the starboard watch moved towards the aft hatch to their mess deck to breakfast and a few hours rest. Captain Beauchamp, his coal black hair blowing forward in the wind, watched the sunrise over the horizon aft of the ship's wake.

"Deck! Ship rounding the point." The look out shouted to alert the quarterdeck.

Captain Beauchamp sprang to the forward quarterdeck rail. "What do you make of her, Mr. Standfield?"

Standfield peered toward the oncoming ship then reported. "Warship, sir, topsail ketch." He focused on the oncoming gunboat. "Well armed and coming fast, sir."

Nate looked around the quarterdeck, searching for one of the midshipmen. "Where is Edwards and Bouchard?" He shouted to no one in particular. Then he noticed the newly promoted quartermaster's mate and motioned to the flag laying folded on the stand near the binnacle. "Mr. Iodice, get the Spanish flag up the halyard, if you please."

He turned at the sound of the first officer rushing up the quarterdeck ladder. "Mr. Kent, we have a guest."

Abe Kent finished buttoning his shirt as he asked. "Where away, sir?"

"Off the larboard bow, Mr. Kent." Nate pointed to the approaching ship.

The halyard squeaked as the Spanish flag rose up the mast. Both men glanced up to see the flag unfold in the brisk breeze. Nate guided Kent toward La Rue. "Mr. Kent, have the men quietly go to quarters and assure they keep their heads below the bulwark." Kent rushed down the ladder to the gundeck as Nate glanced up to the sails. "Mr. La Rue, you better have all the sails taken in except the fighting topsails."

"Aye, monsieur, Captain." La Rue rushed to the forward rail and issued the orders to trim the sails.

Canon fire boomed across the larboard bow dropping a ball three yards to the starboard. A large plumb of water splashed against the starboard bow. Nate watched the ball fly then the splash. "Steer easy, Mr. La Rue, we will let her get along side before we open fire."

Lieutenant La Rue stepped aft to the wheel and motioned for his man, Stewart, to replace Mr. Hall at the wheel.

"I don't mind stay'n with the wheel, Mr. La Rue." Hall protested being replaced by the Irishman.

"It is the larboard watch, Mr. Hall, consider yourself relieved," La Rue moved to watch the approaching ship from a vantage just behind the captain.

"She has broken out the black flag, Captain." Standfield shouted from his perch atop the main mast top yard.

Beauchamp's inner being surged with adrenalin at the anticipation of the coming action. He gripped the rail till his knuckles turned white.

*****

Below decks Shell Levy wiped sweat from his brow as he walked aft. He moved from gun to gun, stopping at each giving encouragement to the gun crews. The men fidgeted with anticipation, anxious for some live action. They stood shirtless, waiting and mopping sweat from their overheated bodies. Levy glanced to the open hatch in anticipation for the order to run out and fire. Nothing. No one came down the hatch. He grabbed a passing powder monkey. "Mr. Wright, have you seen Mr. Bouchard?"

"No, sir, I ain't see'd him all morning." The lad sat his powder bag next to the number four starboard gun, knuckled his forehead to the second officer and ran toward the ladder and down to the magazine.

Levy looked around once more in hopes that his second in command of the lower gundeck had slipped in unnoticed. Then a slamming noise caused him and the gun crew to look aft to the hatch to the main deck. Where light should be shining down was dark as night. They heard the lock pin slide through the hatch cover. He turned and raced toward the forward hatch only to see it slam shut. In total darkness the gun crew's murmer turned to a roar.

"Quiet!" Levy commanded. "We have to figure what is going on and how to get off this gundeck." Silence filled the deck.

*****

Nate stared, watching the topsail ketch come along side. A tall heavy set, mulatto stood on the ketch's quarterdeck, arms crossed, smiling at what Nate was sure the man thought to be an easy prey. Nate slowly raised his hand to give the signal to fling open the gun ports and fire. He glanced down to the gun deck to see the gun captains standing with their arms raised to signal to fire the great guns. Before his eyes the Irish and Frenchmen of the larboard watch abandoned the guns and ran to the arms chest where they pulled swords, boarding axes and knives from the chest. They spread down the deck facing the starboard watch who had remained unarmed at their guns.

"What the hell?" Nate made to move to the ladder to go to the gun deck but felt cold steel against the left side of his neck. He slowly turned to see Lieutenant La Rue holding his sword to his neck. "Mr. La Rue, What is the meaning of this?"

The second lieutenant pressed the sword against the captain's neck; his voice had changed from the high-pitched twang to a deep-throated resonance. "You may call me Captain La Rue of the French Republican Navy." He bent slightly forward to remove Nate's sword. "Such a beautiful sword, Captain

Beauchamp, much too beautiful for an English naval officer." La Rue smiled and drew Nate's attention to the dark skinned man on the quarterdeck of the ketch, now tied to the *Hawk's* side. "You may consider you, your men and the ship *Hawk* prisoners of the Republic of France as well as the pirate Black Caser and his ship the *Royaliste.*

Nate gazed at the pirate ship and her master. "Odd name for a pirate ship in league with a republican country, would you not say, La Rue?"

Chapter Seven

Marooned

For three days the loyal British men endured total darkness with barely room to move, hands bound in irons, unable to see each other as if each man were alone. The heat of the stores hold seemed to intensify with each passing day. The stench of human perspiration and urine filled their nostrils. They remained locked in the dark, damp hold, prisoners in their own ship.

The only light they saw was when, once a day, Bosun Braddock had the hatch opened to toss ship's biscuit down into the blackened storage hold. Hunger caused the men to scramble and fight for a morsel of the worst of the ship's weevil infested biscuit. Next the Irishmen passed down two oak buckets of water to be shared with the one hundred and thirty two officers and men.

Midshipman Edwards gave half of his ration to his pet, Mr. Addington, who ate the sparse ration greedily without any guilt.

The first day the captives were edgy, angry and argumentative at their predicament. By the second day heat and hopelessness overwhelmed them. Each man lay or stood wherever he could find space. Listlessly they lay listening to the mutineers and pirates sing and dance on the deck above, no doubt filled with drink.

"Captain." Abe Kent spoke through the darkness.

"Yes, Abe." Nate hoarsely answered from Kent's left side.

"Oh, sir, I did not know you were so near." He pulled closer to afford them as much privacy as possible. "They sound as if they are taken with drink."

"That they do, Abe," His throat felt raw from lack of moisture.

"Perhaps we could, somehow, coax one of them to open the door on this deck, then we could overcome them and take the ship back." Abe grasped at any chance to escape and regain their ship.

"I think not, Abe, even if we could coax one of them to open the door," He peered into the darkness, searching for Abe's face to no avail; the darkness consumed all possibility of sight. "We are packed in here like so many fish in a barrel, we could not move to take advantage of such an opportunity." He raised his manacle encased wrists to wipe the perspiration from his brow then held his hand in front of his eyes. He could barely make out his hand and could not see his wiggling fingers. "It is best to conserve our energy and make our play when they bring us on deck."

"That could be a long wait." Master McClain volunteered.

"Yes, Mr. McClain, I am aware of that but we have no chance packed in this hold as we are now." He reached into the darkness and touched the old man's arm and squeezed it to give him reassurance.

*****

On the morning of the fourth day Nate heard a commotion on deck. Then he heard the squeak of the capstan turn and the anchor rope rubbing the hawsehole, as it was drawn inboard. Rigging blocks whined as ropes pulled through them and sails cracked and flapped as they were loosened and set free to the wind.

"The ship is getting under way." Shell Levy spoke for the first time.

"Where to, I wonder," Doctor Badeau thought aloud.

"We'll know soon enough, I'll wager." a voice spoke from the dark.

*****

On the morning of the fifth day all sense of forward motion ceased. The *Hawk* wallowed in a rolling sea. The hatch to the stores hold opened. Blinding light shown down the ladder and spilled over the British officers and men as well as their foreign friends imprisoned with them.

A harsh voice called down. "You bloody English scum get yer arses up da ladder, Capt'n La Rue has someth'n ta gives ya." The voice emitted a wicked laugh at his own humor then he sneered down the hatch. "You two grease balls get up here first."

Petty officer Salazar and seaman Dieago Baya glanced to each other then with their binding chains clanking, they climbed the ladder to the deck. Quartermaster's Mate Iodice was next, followed by all the men adjacent to the ladder till an area cleared enough for Captain Beauchamp and the ship's officers to make their way to the ladder and up to the deck.

After days in the black hold the sunlight had a blinding effect on the British navy men. All stood around the deck rubbing their eyes with their manacled hands. As clear sight slowly returned, Nate gazed around the tossing deck. A swell rolled the ship and Nate stutter stepped barely maintaining his balance. He was stiff and his equilibrium was askew after so many days in the cramped hold. A hand reached out to steady him. "I have you, sir." Nate squinted his eyes to see his Italian clerk, Luigi, hold his arm firmly.

"Thank you, Mr. Colavecchio." Nate stretched, pulling his stiff muscles.

"Captain, Monsieur Beauchamp." La Rue called down from the quarterdeck.

"Captain!" Shell Levy called from behind several men. "That is the voice I heard at the inn that night."

Nate made to rush the quarterdeck to attack La Rue but the French and Irish guards held him back.

"I am afraid your mission to La Florida has been superceded, monsieur." La Rue smiled down at the Royal Navy men in their tired dirty state.

For the first time Nate's eyes were adjusted to the sunlight enough for him to look about. The pirate ship *Royaliste* was no longer tied to the *Hawk*'s side. Nate rubbed his eyes, then searched the horizon for the ship only to find no sign of her. The strain on his eyes, after so many days in the dark hold, caused his eyes to water. He rubbed his eyes once more, then looked up to La Rue on the quarterdeck. La Rue grinned from ear to ear in his triumph over the British and their captain. To his left the Irish traitor Braddock stood with his new master. It was what was between them that made Nate's mouth drape open. Jasper, in his best uniform stood with decanter and two glasses on a silver tray.

"Ah! Monsieur Beauchamp, I see you recognize my new servant," La Rue gave a throaty laugh. "I must thank you for training him so well." He reached and took a glass from the silver tray then nodded for Braddock to do the same. When La Rue and Braddock turned back to face him, Nate thought he saw Jasper's left eye wink.

The Frenchman slightly rocked back and forth on his heels, gloating in the success over the British. "If we can teach this black beast to communicate in French, I may take him with me when I triumphantly return to France." He reached his glass high into the air, a toast to himself. "I shall be a hero of the people for preventing you from interfering with the recovery of *San Pedro's* gold." He leaned forward to drive his point home. "Gold! Monsieur, gold that will see Ireland finally break free of the British chains of oppression. Free to take her rightful place at the side of France."

"What do you intend to do with us La Rue?" Captain Beauchamp demanded.

Captain La Rue ceased his dissertation on Irish freedom and his expected hero's welcome to France. "Captain La Rue to you. Have you no manners to address your superior so?" La Rue's smile faded, replaced with and angry scowl.

The *Hawk's* rightful captain remained silent and continued to glare at the Frenchman.

"Well, we knew you to be a crude man of low birth." La Rue sneered.

Abe Kent made to push past his captain to get at the Frenchman but was quickly checked by Beauchamp on one side and Levy on the other. "Not now, Abe, our time will come." Nate nudged the first officer back behind him.

"Here is your new command, Captain Beauchamp." La Rue raised his hand to the larboard. The British prisoner's eyes followed the Frenchman's outstretched arm. A large island with white sandy beaches and thick forest lay off *Hawk's* larboard side. He continued, "Fiddler's Island shall be your prison to command, Monsieur."

"You intend to maroon us, sir?" Nate glared at the Frenchman.

"Maroon, such a harsh word, monsieur." The Frenchman noticed his empty glass and held it for Jasper to refill. "Pirates maroon people, Monsieur Captain." He sipped from the refilled glass. "I think of it as an opportunity for you to live a little longer." La Rue threw the glass to the deck, shattering it, then snatched his sword out of the scabbard and leaned over the rail, pointing it at Nate. "Or would you rather die here and now?"

The British seamen nervously mumbled at the implication made by the Frenchman. Nate calmly continued to glair at the Frenchman.

"Enough of this!" shouted La Rue. He glanced to Bosun Braddock. "Load them in the boats."

Bosun Braddock nodded to the French and Irish guards who then began pushing and shoving the prisoners to the larboard bulwark and the waiting boats. Irish seaman Nolan shoved Topman Bobby Mantell in the back with the muzzle of his musket. Mantell swung around and clubbed Nolan's face with his clenched fist, knocking him to the deck.

Mantell sprung forward into a French guard, wrapped his hands around the man's neck and rode him to the deck, squeezing and choking as they fell.

The British prisoners rushed to attack the guards but were quickly subdued with a counter attack from the armed guards. Flanagan rushed to the two men fighting on the deck. The French guard turned blue and gasped for breath under Mantell's choking grip. Flanagan raised his musket and slammed the butt against Mantell's head. The American went limp. Flanagan shoved the unconscious Mantell off the gasping Frenchman with his boot. "Drag this Yankee over to his British masters."

Doctor Badeau pushed through the prisoners and leaned down to tend Mantell's wound.

"You!" La Rue shouted down to the deck. "My good doctor." He scanned the crowded prisoners, searching for familiar faces. "And the rest of the French Royalist will be kept on board and taken back to France in chains, to be tried for treason."

Nate shoved men aside and stepped to the front of his men. "Captain La Rue, these men have done France no wrong." He glanced back to the Frenchmen standing among the prisoners then back to the quarterdeck. "They only sought a different life than your republic offers."

"Captain Beauchamp, even you must admit serving on an enemy's warship is a treasonable offense." La Rue glanced down to Bosun

Braddock. "Seize the traitors to the revolution and throw them in the cable tier."

Braddock pushed through the prisoners pulling Frenchmen from the group. He nodded to Gregory Campbell then to Doctor Badeau. Campbell took the doctor's elbow and lifted him from tending Mantell. "Come along peaceful like, doctor." Doctor Badeau stood as told on the ship's main hatch and watched his comrades pulled from the group of prisoners. Master Gunner Folliot snatched his arm from Braddock's grip and proudly marched out of the grouped prisoners to stand with the French Royalist on the main hatch.

Braddock pulled the fighting and kicking Midshipman Bouchard to the front of the prisoners and shoved him down at the feet of Master Gunner Folliot.

"You can not take me back to France, I am a serving British naval officer." The boy cried.

Folliot lifted the boy by his elbow and dusted his coat. "Stand here, Monsieur Bouchard, like the man you have shown yourself to be."

Nate shoved Braddock aside and shouted to La Rue. "Captain La Rue! Do not take the lad, surely you can show compassion for this young boy."

"You jest, Monsieur Beauchamp," La Rue gripped the quarterdeck rail and leaned forward. "He is of royal blood. Of all these men he will most certainly loose his head." He straightened up and flipped his hand toward the waiting boats. "Load these dogs into the boats."

The guards pushed the prisoners down the rope ladders attached to the side of the ship. Nate watched the boats slowly fill, then with his sailors at the oars and four armed Irish guards, each filled boat pulled away from the side and hove too while the next boat filled. After the last longboat filled He slung his leg over the bulwark to make his climb down the ladder into the boat.

"Wait!" Shouted La Rue as he walked to the flag locker and pulled out the British ensign and handed it to a French quartermaster. "Here is your flag, Beauchamp. We have no need for it on this French ship." His grin was one of wicked triumph. Glaring at the Frenchman, Nate took the flag, tucked it in his blouse and then lowered himself to the waiting longboat.

*****

Beauchamp stood up, cautiously balancing, careful to prevent tipping the overloaded longboat. He heard Mr. Edward's monkey cry out from the next longboat to his right. Glancing over he saw one of the Irish guards holding Mr. Addington's head under his foot. Edwards pleaded with the guard to release the monkey. The guard shoved Edwards back to his seat and laughed wildly as he applied pressure to the little animal's head. Finally Gregory Campbell, senior guard of the boat, shoved the guard away from the monkey and the animal scurried to Daniel Edward's lap where he laid whimpering. With the commotion died down on the other longboat, Nate slowly moved forward between the English oarsmen then glanced up at the armed Irish guards watching his every move. He made the decision to go no further. “Mr. McClain, would you please inspect the stores the mutineers have given us.

Taking exception to his men being referred to as mutineers, Flanagan hollered, “Irish Patriots! Beauchamp, fight’n fer liberty, now take yer seat and shut up.”

Fourth lieutenant Foster sprung from his seat, swinging at Flanagan’s head. “Don’t talk to a British Naval officer that way, you Irish scum!”

Flanagan dodged Foster’s outstretched arms, swinging the butt of his musket into Foster’s stomach as he crouched. Foster doubled over and fell to the bottom of the boat, striking his head against the gunnel as he dropped. Leaning over Foster’s collapsed torso, Flanagan raised his musket to deliver a final blow to the fallen officer.

“Flanagan!” Beauchamp jumped up from his seat, glaring at the angry Irishman. “Belay that and return to your duty.”

Years of serving under British officers and various naval ships had trained Flanagan to obey without question. He resumed his position guarding the prisoners before he realized he was in charge. “I’ll have no more of that! You British pigs had best mind yer selves or I’ll be forced ta take action against ya.”

Nate resumed his seat in the stern of the longboat and watched as the boats pulled ashore. The nose of the longboats each slid up onto the white sandy beach where the armed Irishmen leapt from the small fleet of longboats and circled the British with weapons at the ready. Mr. Addington escaped from Midshipman Edward's arms and raced up the beach, then disappeared into the trees at the jungle's edge. Edwards sprang from the boat to catch the monkey but two guards forced him back into the boat with their muskets.

The British of the *Hawk* sat steadfast in the longboats staring at the Irish guards surrounding them.

"Everyone stay as ya are till I tells ya ta get out of yer boat." Flanagan marched up the line of beached longboats repeating his order then back to the east end of the boats and stood to the side of the boat carrying the *Hawk's* senior officers. "You gent'l men get out o' da boat real slow like and march yer selves up the beach to da trees."

First Levy, then Kent stepped over the gunnel, fiddler crabs scurried to their holes in the sand. The other senior officers stepped out, and then finally Captain Beauchamp followed them. They splashed ashore and marched ten yards up the beach and stopped.

Flanagan came up the beach with two unarmed guards. He held his musket on the officers while the two Irish guards unlocked their chains. Steven Stuart snatched Beauchamp's arms and unlocked the chains on his wrists. "If'n it were up ta me I'd leave the chains on this bunch and that's fer sure."

"Shut up, Stuart, an do as yer told." Flanagan ordered.

Kent pointed to the water keg and a small bundle of stores in the bow of the longboat. "What about the stores, Flanagan?"

"Never you mind, we'll unload them once ye are all ashore, now get yer selves up the beach to the tree line."

"Let's move on lads, there is nothing we can do to change our situation at present." Nate turned and moved to the tree line as officers reluctantly trailed behind him.

When the officers reached the large palms and thick brush they stopped and stood watching the remaining boats unload. Each longboat unloaded one at a time, the same as the first. As the men from the last boat reached the trees and brush half the Irishmen laid down their weapons and stacked the stores at the front of each longboat. Flanagan signaled and the guards boarded the boats, shoved off and pulled for the *Hawk*.

Flanagan stood in the stern of his longboat, made a speaking trumpet with his hands and yelled a last message to the marooned men. "By da time ya gets back ta England, Ireland will be free," then added. "If ya live." He gave a wicked laugh at his own joke then sat down and urged the oarsmen to pull harder for the *Hawk*.

Nate watched as the longboats were pulled aboard *Hawk*. The Irish and French laughed and pointed to the marooned British men standing and watching as they went about the business of getting the *Hawk* under sail.

"Damn them! Damn their bloody souls!" Kent shouted taking his frustration out on the white beach sand he kicked.

Levy and Edwards tended to Foster's wounded head while Nate and the remaining men watched as *Hawk* sailed around the tip of the island and out of sight.

"What do we do now, Captain?"

Nate glanced to his side and the voice of his clerk. "Mr. Colavecchio, first we take care of our sustenance water, food and shelters." He turned and scanned the sea where his ship had laid off shore." The bright sun glared down on where the *Hawk* had hove too and sent a blinding reflection back to taunt him. "We will find a way to get off this Island," Nate looked the clerk in the eye. "Then, Mr. Colavecchio, I will hunt down and kill that man."

*****

For the first time Nate studied the jungle. "There must be water with all this forestation." He walked along the line of palm trees and brush. "And food on such a lush island." He called to the first officer, "Mr. Kent."

Abe Kent scurried to his side. "Sir?"

"Inventory the stores and see what the Frenchman has left us." They walked back to the men waiting near the stores. "Mr. levy and Major Scarlet divide half the men into groups and forage for water and anything edible." He beckoned the midshipman to his side. "Mr. Edwards take two men and scout the jungle for a path to the top of that hill." He pointed up to the rock-covered top of the hill towering above the center of the island.

Lieutenant Foster held his hand over his head wound as he approached. "Sir, What can I do to help our situation?"

Nate guided the young fourth officer to the shade of some unknown variety of tropical tree. "I have quite enough volunteers at the moment, Howard," Urging Foster to be seated in the shade. "You need to rest right now." He walked back to where the remaining men waited for him to dish them up some task that needed doing. "I'll need you later, Mr. Foster," Calling back to the young officer.

"Mr. McClain, set some of these men to finding firewood." He scanned the area. "Locate an area we can use as a camp, preferably some clearing back in the jungle and away from passing ships."

"Don't we need a passing ship to see our fires to rescue us, sir?" An alarmed Master McClain asked.

"You forget these waters are well traveled by French warships, my friend." He squeezed the old man's shoulder. "I want to get off this island as much as you but not as a prisoner of war."

McClain blushed and nodded. "Aye, sir, I were in such a lather ta get out of here I did not consider the consequences. Sorry, sir."

"No need to apologize, Mr. McClain. We will all feel better with a deck under our feet." Captain Beauchamp turned at his name being called by Sinbad, the midshipmen's Moroccan.

"Captain, Boy Daniel say come, boy find path up hill." The out of breath Moroccan spilled Mr. Edward's message in broken English.

"Mr. McClain, take charge and carry out your duties." Beauchamp yelled to the ship's master as he followed Sinbad to the path."

*****

The climb up the hill had taken them an hour and a half. The path was overgrown with vegetation but had undoubtedly been well used at some time in the past. Many of these Virgin Islands had been colonized at one time or another. The settlement here must have failed for some reason or perhaps native Indians originally made this trail. There was no way of knowing.

Beauchamp leaned against a smooth large rock. He braced his feet on the ledge and shaded his eyes from the bright tropical sun. The waters were vast and ran quickly down the passage between Fiddler's Island and the islands in the distance. *Too far to swim and a contrary current for a raft. Even if we made it to one of the other islands there is no sign they are inhabited.* "Let us have a look from the west side of the island, Mr. Edwards."

Young Edwards led the way around the crown of the rocky promontory, pulling loose dead brush and kicking loose rocks from the path as he slowly made his way to the west edifice. Edwards, who had worked his way ahead of Nate and the other two men, came running back half way and excitedly shouted. "Oh! Sir, it is beautiful on the other side, hurry come see."

Nate picked up his pace as the boy rushed ahead. "I am sure it will still be there when," Nate was overcome by the beautiful before him. "...We get there, Mr. Edwards." He continued as he drank in the luscious greens of the foliage and bright orange, red and white flowers which sprinkled downward to end at a white sandy beach and a crescent shaped dark blue lagoon.

Half way down the hill a wide clear pool of water slowly released a waterfall some thirty feet down to a small stream that wound through the green jungle to empty past the white shore into the lagoon.

Able Seaman Jenkins and Sinbad stood with mouths agape at such beauty.

"Oh, sir." Edwards pleaded with his captain. "Could you please have our camp on this side of the island?"

"I am afraid not, Daniel." Nate patted the excited lad's back.

"But, sir, it is so beautiful, and there is water and fruit and..." The excited young Daniel Edwards was stopped short.

"Daniel, the main sea lanes are off the coast of the other side of the island." Nate gazed down the beautiful hillside, past the pool and waterfall to the blue lagoon. "If we are to signal a British ship it will be on the other side of the island."

"I suppose you are correct, sir, but it is so very lovely here." Daniel smiled to his captain.

"Yes, it is, Mr. Edwards, however we must be about the business of setting up our camp." Beauchamp started back down the path to the other side of the promontory. "Why don't you and your Sinbad go back to the beach and draw some biscuit and jerky then return here and stand watch?" They headed down the path to the beach. "You never know when a fast British frigate will come sailing down Drake's Channel."

"Yes, sir!" Edwards knuckled his forehead and raced down the path with Sinbad on his heels.

Nate and seaman Jenkins stepped down the path and around a frangipani shrub and were almost knocked over by Edwards and Sinbad racing from a clearing to the right side of the trail. "Oh, excuse me, sir, I did not expect you to reach the camp so soon."

"Camp?" Nate asked as he peered around the frangipani bush to see Mr. McClain had established the camp several hundred yards up the path from the beach. The new camp was full of activity and seemed to be well on the way to being established. "Mr. Edwards I will send a relief in four hours, keep a good watch on the channel and alert me immediately should you see a ship."

"Aye, sir." Edwards lifted his hat in salute and Sinbad knuckled his forehead as he passed to follow the midshipman up the path.

Beauchamp walked into the camp and glanced around. He was impressed that the men could accomplish so much in so little time. Men sat around campfires while others moved about placing various fruits in separate piles. Sharpened sticks were stacked against a mango tree, ready to be used as spears should the group need to be defended.

Abe Kent approached grinning. "Everything we need to survive is on this island." He pointed to the gathered mangoes, bananas and berries. To the left some kind of large tropical fish were mounted on thick poles roasting over a fire. He glanced back to Captain Beauchamp turning his grin into a frown. "Everything we need with the exception of water." Kent pointed to an unseen location high up the hill." Mr. Levy did find a stagnate rain pool up the slope, but it is undrinkable without boiling and we have not devised a means to fabricate a pot to boil it in.

Nate indicated the path he had recently descended. "Plenty of water on the other side of the island, a large pool and a waterfall for washing in," He glanced to the stacked stores. "Did the mutineers give us the means to carry water?"

"We can use the two water kegs when they empty however, it will mean several trips to refill them with so many men" Kent and Beauchamp walked toward the stacked stores.

"Just what do we have in the way of stores?" Beauchamp asked.

"Sir, they gave us little to survive with." He ran down a memorized cursory list of stores. "Two machetes, a barrel of ship's biscuit, three heads of cheese." He glanced to the stacked stores then back to the captain as he continued. "A few blankets, not near enough for our large party of men, a half keg of beef and nothing to warm it in." Abe turned to glance at a group of seamen carrying coconuts. "Assorted small items, but not near enough to sustain this many men."

They walked to the shade of what Nate thought to be a papaya tree. He snapped a pear shaped fruit from the tree, examined the golden yellow skin, rubbed the fruit on his sleeve then took a bite. "Mmm, quite good, Abe, try one."

Abe scanned the tree for just the right one and snapped it from the branch. He repeated Nate's method of examination and cleaning on his sleeve then took a large bite. Juice ran down his chin from an over full mouth. His attempts to praise the fruit were thwarted by the large, luscious amount he had taken in his first bite. Abe grinned at his inability to communicate and Nate nodded concurrence at what he surmised to be the first officer's opinion.

Nate pointed to the perimeter of the camp. "Even though we only have the two machetes and the spears you have fashioned, we best build some kind of fortification to slow any attack should we be found out by the French." He strode out into the sun and scanned the camp till he located the carpenter. "Give one of the machetes to Mr. Papas and his mates, perhaps they can fashion water buckets from a tree trunk."

Kent swallowed the remaining papaya and asked. "Should we not try to build a boat or raft, sir?"

Nate's eyes continued to scan the camp. "I think not, Abe." They walked to the path and down the several yards to the beach, Nate talking as they walked. "We could never build a raft to accommodate more than a few men." He nodded to the sea flowing past the island. "The currents of Sir Frances Drake Channel are strong and may push the raft into enemy hands." Picking up a rock, Nate threw it as hard as he could out into the surf. "I think it best to keep a good lookout," He turned and looked up to the hilltop. "From the top of that hill our lookouts can see for miles to the East and West, all we have to do is wait until a British ship comes close enough to see our signal." He saw questions in Abe's eyes about his intensions. "Abe even if a far off ship appears to be British built it could have been captured by the French. We need for a ship to come close enough to see its flag." Placing his arm around his friend's shoulder he guided him back up the path to the camp. "It is best this way. Armed with only spears and two machetes we would stand little chance against a well armed enemy."

*****

Over the next two weeks Captain Beauchamp kept the officers and men busy building the fortifications, gathering fruit, catching fish and fetching water from the deep pool on the other side of the island. It was a challenge to keep the men active and their minds off the fact that they were marooned with small hope of rescue. The officers maintained shipboard routines for the men as a way to maintain discipline on the tropical island. The men were divided into new larboard and starboard watches for security and work details. Mornings were filled with the chores required to sustain the ship's company. Noontime was set aside for personal activities such as swimming in the surf or resting from the tropical heat of the midday, which was almost unbearable on the men from a country that bordered the North Sea. Evenings were spent singings songs and telling the tales seamen are prone to share. All was as well as could be expected under their predicament. Just the same, Captain Beauchamp kept a weather eye on the wellness of the ship's company and the prospect of rescue.

Nate and his senior officers sat on logs before a morning campfire having their breakfast of mangoes, bananas, and papaya chased with a dipper they passed around of the last water from the two casks. They glanced up at the noise made by the work detail preparing to shove off to visit the pool on the far side of the hill to replenish their water supply.

Master McClain flung a banana peel over his shoulder and wiped his mouth with his shirtsleeve. "Ya know, I never thought I would be tired of fruit."

"Aye, me too." Called Sergeant Major Christmas. "What I wouldn't give for some good o'l ship's pork right now."

Purser Pearse gave a hardy laugh. "Yeah, ten years in the keg. Ha! Ha!"

The officers continued to chew their fruit in silence but all stared at the man responsible for feeding them aboard the *Hawk*.

"Weren't my fault," The purser whined. "I had to take what the Vitualling Board issued me." He stood up and moved away from the group looking back to see any sign of compassion from the officers. Seeing none, he moved to the petty officer's fire but was ignored and eventually wandered off by himself.

"Shouldn't be so hard on Mr. Pearse ," the captain declared. "He does the best he can with what is issued to him and I have served with far worse pursers."

"Oh. He ain't so bad, sir," Howard Foster chimed in. "We just have to keep O'l Pearse in check or he will think we are fond of him." They all laughed at Foster's remark.

*****

Captain Beauchamp, with trousers rolled up and stockings and boots removed, waded through the shallow water fishing with the spear Diego Baya had made for him. He waded slowly thirty feet behind and shoreward of the Spanish seamen, Baya and young Anthony Ortagus. The water was cloudy from the small waves, which lapped the beach. Between the receding waves Nate saw the mullet skimming through the shallows. He lunged his spear at the passing school of fish but missed all. The two grinning Spaniards kept their heads lowered looking for fish to spear but occasionally cut their eyes to the inept fisherman behind them. Young Ortagus lunged his spear forward, moved over the spear sticking in the bottom of the shallow water, slid his hand under the fish he speared and raised it out of the water. Daniel Edwards raced to Ortagus, holding open the straw basket Sinbad made to hold the catch. Anthony flipped the fish into the basket and Daniel quickly placed the cover on the basket.

Captain Beauchamp stood watching the lucky fishermen. "This is not for me." He shook his head and departed the water, giving his spear to Topman Mantell who was watching the fishermen. "Here Mr. Mantell, perhaps you will be more skilled than I." He looked out to the shallows to see Diego Baya excitedly holding a fish for all to see. "If we depend on me to catch a fish, we will all starve." Nate returned Mantell's grin with his own smile as he walked further up the beach to fetch his stockings and boots.

"Captain! Captain! Captain!" Mr. Foster came racing down the path and up to the captain.

Nate reached out catching the officer, preventing his momentum from carrying Foster past him and into the water. "What has alarmed you so, Mr. Foster?"

"A ship, sir! A bloody ship." The excited lieutenant shouted.

Nate glanced past the rollers to an empty horizon.

"Not there, sir." Foster pulled the captain around and pointed up the path. "In the lagoon on the other side of the island!"

Beauchamp stooped over, pulled on his stockings and boots over his wet, sandy feet, then followed the excited fourth lieutenant. Up the path they went, passing officers and men who correctly waited for the captain to climb the hill first. Half way up the hill Nate turned to Mr. Levy. "Best keep these men back, Shell, till we see who these fellows are."

Beauchamp and Foster reached the apex to see Abe Kent peering around the edge of the large rock that led to the path the water detail had created to take them down to the stoop above the waterfall. Kent glanced back, then waved Beauchamp forward. He stepped aside to allow the captain to assume his vantage point. "She is a brig, sir!" His excitement at seeing the ship had caused him to loose his breath. He paused slightly, took a deep breath of air and continued. "Looks American built, sir, see the..." Kent leaned over Nate's right shoulder and pointed down to the vessel in the lagoon. "See the spanker on her aft mast?" He withdrew his arm and stood straight, proud of his ship identification skill. "She is an American snow."

Nate concentrated his focus on the men now debarking the ship and climbing down into a longboat. "She may have begun life as an American snow, Mr. Kent, but unless I am mistaken those are the red coats of British marines in that longboat pulling for shore."

"Oh my God, we're saved." Kent gasped.

Shell Levy had just joined two senior officers in time to hear the captain's remark as he glanced around the hilltop. "And I was just getting used to this place."

Beauchamp and Kent glanced back at Lieutenant Levy's grinning face and returned his with grins of their own.

"We best find a way down to the beach, Mr. Kent." Nate pointed to where the path ended just past the waterfall.

*****

Captain Beauchamp, Abe Kent and Shell Levy arrived at the beach as the seamen from the brig were dipping water into their last water barrel from the stream. The remaining men of the *Hawk* were ordered to remain behind so as to not alarm the seamen on the beach. The officers watched for a short time, giving Nate time to choose a method to approach the group without getting them shot. The ship's two marines walked up and down the beach watching the jungle for some unanticipated danger.

"Stay here till I call you," Nate raised his hands and slowly stepped onto the beach.

"Here, now!" The marine corporal quickly lowered his musket to point at Nate's mid section and moved rapidly to take command of the stranger approaching from the jungle. "Who might you be?"

Nate moved slowly toward the marine. "I am Commander Nathan Beauchamp." He lowered his hands. "Captain of the *HMS Hawk*."

"And I'm the king of bloody Spain." The corporal flipped his musket, indicating for Nate to raise his hands. "Get them 'ands back in the air."

The Marine private deserted the seamen filling the water casks to reinforce the corporal. "Looks like a bloody pirate ta me, corporal."

The corporal briefly glanced to the approaching private then back to the man now standing still with his hands over his head. "What would you know about how a pirate looks, Private Smith?" He nervously blinked at Nate and used his musket to motion Nate to move toward the longboat. "We best take this fellow to Captain Nobbs."

"Nobbs?" Nate grinned at the name of his friend. "You don't mean Simon Nobbs, do you corporal?"

The corporal was surprised the stranger knew his captain. "You know Captain Nobbs?"

"Yes, corporal, we served together earlier in the spring. He flipped his hand at the anchored brig; of course he commanded the *Dart* back then.

The corporal's face turned white. "By God, I think ye're tell'n the truth." He brought his musket to his side and stood at attention. "Corporal George Nelson, *HMS Drake*, at yer service, sir."

"Not related to Admiral Nelson, Commander-in-Chief of the Mediterranean, are you, Corporal Nelson?" Nate teased.

"Oh, how I wish, your honor," The corporal glanced to the anchored *Drake*. "Me life would be much better than guarding this here watering detail." Shaking his head in disappointment.

The marine private timidly stood behind Corporal Nelson. "I see'd pirates one time."

Corporal Nelson gave the private a sideways look of disgust. "And where might that be, Private Smith?"

Private Smith looked down to his feet and lowly mumbled. "It were on the dock at Kingston." He grinned and rolled his eyes up to look at the corporal and the captain. "They was kinda hang'n around, at the time."

"You are a rogue, Tyson Smith." Corporal Nelson reached out to cuff the private's ear but Smith ducked and giggled as he slipped over to help the watering detail.

Corporal Nelson watched the private jokingly tease one of the watering detail seamen. "That man will be the death of me, your honor."

"I can see that, Corporal Nelson." Beauchamp glanced to the edge of the jungle and pointed to where he had come on the beach. "I have two officers with me, corporal."

Waving Kent and Levy forward. "They will need to come with us to greet Captain Nobbs.

*****

"Boat retuning, sir," The duty quartermaster called to Captain Simon Nobbs as he and acting First Officer Duncan MacKensie leaned over a chart spread atop the binnacle.

Captain Nobbs continued studying the chart of the Sir Frances Drake Channel. "Bout time they returned, I am anxious to get the ship under way."

"Water detail ain't on the boat, sir. Someone else is." The quartermaster continued to watch the approaching boat.

Captain Nobbs and Lieutenant MacKensie walked toward the quartermaster to see for themselves. "Who else could possibly be in the water boat, Quartermaster Ingalls?" Nobbs called out as he and MacKensie drew alongside the mystified quartermaster who answered. "Pirates, sir."

MacKensie rested his hand on his Samurai sword. "He appears to be correct, Simon, All they need is earrings and a monkey."

Simon Nobbs cut his eyes to MacKensie and his snide remark then called to the boat. "Boat, ahoy!"

Corporal Nelson stood in the bow of the boat, cupped his hands and shouted. "Captain Beauchamp, *HMS Hawk*."

Simon and Duncan looked at each other and mouthed in unison. "Nate!" As they rushed to the entry port to greet their old friend.

Chapter Eight

In Search of Hawk

Nate sat in front of Simon Nobbs desk telling the *Drake's* captain and first officer how the French spies and Irish Rebels took his ship and marooned him, his officers and men.

"Where do you think this fellow will take the *Hawk*?" Simon asked.

Nate told the *Drake's* officers about his orders to prevent the pirates and Irish Rebels from retrieving the *San Pedro's* gold. "I would think La Rue would take the *Hawk* to where the *San Pedro* is being salvaged to boast of his success and demonstrate that the British threat has been eliminated." Nate rose from his seat. "Simon I must know what your orders are for the *Drake's* immediate future."

Simon slid his chair back from the desk and looked up to study Nate's eyes. "We are on independent duty for the next two months."

"Independent duty?" Nate queried.

Simon retrieved his orders from the desk drawer and handed them to the senior officer. "We are to inflict damage to the enemy wherever we find him."

Nate placed both hands on the desk and leaned towards Captain Nobbs. "Simon, I know where we can inflict severe damage on the enemy and serve our King best."

Simon and Duncan were transfixed on Beauchamp's words. "On the *Hawk*, in a hidden place, I have orders from Admiral, Sir George Montague, as representative of the First Lord of the Admiralty which gives me the authority to obtain assistance from any and all His Majesty's ships, officers and military." Nate lied. "I need you and the *Drake* to assist me in completing my mission."

"Well, sir, I suppose we will have to take you to Florida so you can show us the document." Simon rose smiling and shook Nate's hand. "I and the *Drake* are at your service, Commander."

"Thank you, Captain Nobbs." Beauchamp turned towards the cabin door. "First thing we must do is retrieve my men from the other side of the island."

Duncan MacKensie jumped from his seat. "I shall be happy to take care of that task for you, Captain Beauchamp." He glanced to Levy and Kent. "If these fellows will assist."

"Most certainly." Spoke Kent as he and a nodding Levy followed Duncan out the cabin door.

Simon took the decanter from the cupboard with two glasses and held them up to Nate, who nodded his agreement to a morning drink. "I see you surround yourself with good officers once again, Nate."

Beauchamp looked at the closed door his senior officers had just closed behind them. "I am afraid this time I was fortunate," Lifting his glass in response to Simon's toast. "Two out of three is not so bad." They clinked glasses and toasted the King and officers at sea.

Nate set his glass down and waved off the offer for another. "Speaking of good officers, I see you have a fine one in Duncan MacKensie." He adjusted his coat after flapping the lapels to move some air around his torso cooling himself in the hot cabin. "What happened to his ship *Valliant*?"

Simon pored himself another glass of claret, then set the decanter on the desk. "She ran up on a reef while chasing a smuggler last month." He sipped the claret then continued. "He is awaiting another command and volunteered to sail with me as my premier for this cruise."

"Any prospects for him in the near future?" Nate inquired.

"There is an American smuggler taken off the coast of Nevis last month. She is a new brig which was carrying arms to Martinique on her first cruise." Simon turned his glass upside down and grinned at Nate. "A small habit I acquired from drinking contests in my youth."

Nate smiled and nodded.

Simon continued. "She was taken in the service by the admiral at Barbados and has been promised to Duncan."

"I am sure Duncan will put her to good use for the service." Beauchamp resumed his seat and shoved his empty glass across the desk. "Perhaps I will have that second drink after all."

*****

Captains Beauchamp and Nobbs leaned over the charts of the Virgin Islands and the larger islands between their present position and the Spanish Florida Keys.

Simon ran his fingers in a circular motion around the center of the chart. "Now that I have had time to think about this Frenchman, he has no reason to hurry to the Keys; now that he believes the danger to the salvage of the *San Pedro* has been eliminated." He ran his fingers from Tortola in the Virgin Islands, up the chart, past Spanish Puerto Rico, then on to the British Bahamas. "He could linger anywhere around these islands to take a prize or two." Glancing to Nate to see if he concurred. "From what you tell me, the *Hawk* carries a powerful broadside in a hull that looks harmless."

"Yes, Simon. He could snap up half the ships in this area before a King's ship could be sent to stop him." Beauchamp stood staring at the empty horizon. "My first duty is to stop the salvage of the *San Pedro.*" He glanced back to the chart. "Naturally it would be most gratifying to retake the *Hawk* in the process." He smiled to his friend.

"Well, sir, what say we head west?" Simon's eyes looked to the reddish glow of the west horizon.

Nate grinned at his accommodating friend then looked forward to the setting sun. "West! It shall be Captain Nobbs."

*****

With the *Hawk's* men and officers available to him, Captain Nobbs established the *Drake's* watches so that each officer and seaman alike stood four hours on duty with eight hours off; unheard of in a navy with most ships under-manned. Still the little ship was over manned; crowded was a more accurate term.

With not enough space in the little brig to accommodate so many men, off duty men were often in the way of the on duty seamen when it came time to make a change of sail. Soon, the off duty topmen found it more comforting to go aloft to assist the duty section. The result was the quickest change to sails in the fleet. Nate watched the seamen race up the shrouds as if they were in a contest to see who could lower or raise sails the quickest.

"If all His Majesty's ships could effect sail change as quickly as the *Drake,* we could out maneuver all our enemies into submission in quick order," he said, speaking to no one in particular.

He heard a thud hit the deck behind him and turned to see Abe Kent standing over a small canvas sack. "What is this, Mr. Kent?" He queried.

"Mr. Pearse found something in this sack we overlooked when we inventoried the stores on the island." Abe opened the bag and pulled out the *Hawk's* oiled skin dispatch pouch, which was used to send reports and dispatches to superior officers. "Something odd is in this pouch, captain." Abe replied holding the pouch for Nate to take.

Nate took the pouch and untied the flap, then reached inside and pulled out a small bottle and set it on the binnacle. Reaching in again he retrieved what felt like a large book. "The *Hawk's* logbook." He exclaimed as he set the book next to the bottle, trying to understand their meaning. "Why would someone place these in with our stores?"

"Don't know, captain," Abe pulled the cork from the bottle and sniffed. "Rum!" He reached the open bottle over for Nate to sniff."

Nate dropped the dispatch bag to the deck and grabbed for the bottle. CLANK! The pouch hit the deck. Bending over and retrieving the pouch Nate dove in his hand and pulled out the jewel encased letter opener from his desk. Turning the letter opener over in his hand, the sunlight reflected off the blade. He drew the opener near to examine something on the blade he thought he saw. "Look at this, Abe. Something is scratched into the blade."

Abe took the opener and slowly rotated it as he tried to make out what the scratches were. "Rom K," he called out to Nate. As he rotated the blade again, he studied the additional marks near the tip. "JB." He questioningly looked up at Beauchamp. "What does all this mean?"

Nate glanced about the deck. *What can all this mean?* His roving eyes stopped when they settled on his clerk, Luigi, sitting in one of the longboats secured at midships. "Mr. Colavecchio," He called. As the clerk raised his head upon hearing his name called, Nate waved for him to come to him. "I wonder if we could borrow you a moment?"

Luigi stood in the longboat; his trousers were rolled above his knees. He had been soaking his feet in the water carried in the longboat, which kept the harsh tropical sun from opening the boats seams while it was stored aboard the ship. Luigi rolled his trousers down and reached for his shoes and stockings. Nate almost called out that the shoes would not be necessary, but remembered how hot the deck would be on the man's feet, so he continued to study the items from the dispatch bag while he waited for the clerk to arrive.

"Ah! Mr. Colavecchio, I wonder if you could take a look at these items found in the dispatch pouch and venture a guess as to their meaning." Nate stepped aside to provide space for Luigi to examine the items.

Luigi lifted the bottle and sniffed, then glanced at the cover of the logbook. *HMS Hawk*, running his fingers over the words. He glanced to Nate and Abe to ascertain if this was a test or some kind of English game. They had a determined look about them.

"Oh, Mr. Colavecchio, the pouch also contained this letter opener with words scratched into it." Abe held out the opener.

Luigi took the opener, turned it around several times studying the scratching on the blade. Then glanced down to the bottle and back to the blade. He retrieved the bottle and sniffed it once more. With a smile he said, "I have not been a good teacher." And then shook his head slowly. "Or perhaps he was not a good student," he said, then grinned and almost chuckled at the two bewildered officers.

The impatient Abe Kent called out. "What is it man? What have you discovered?" he demanded.

Luigi drew himself up and displayed his most professional manner. "This is from a student of mine." And slowly shook his head in animated disappointment. "One who learns fast but not quite well enough." Abe placed his hands on his hips, a clear show of his disapproval of the man dragging out his findings. Nate watched and listened, allowing Luigi his theatrics. Luigi held the blade of the opener for Nate to see as he ran his finger under the first word. "Rom!" Nate and Abe stared with arched eyebrows and questioning faces. Seeing their lack of understanding, Luigi moved his finger and pointed to the open bottle on the binnacle, then back to the first word on the blade. "Rum!" He stated.

"Oh! I see." Abe smiled at the demonstrated link between the work and the contents of the bottle.

Luigi moved to the next letter scratched on the blade. "'*K*'. I do not know what it means but it is the letter '*K*'." Nate and Abe's eyes pleaded for a solution to the mystery. Luigi looked from Nate to Abe. "I can not tell you anything more." He placed his fingers under the remaining two letters on the blade. "Except he told me his name was Jasper Beauchamp and these are his initials."

A bright light was shining in Nate's eyes. "But of course!" He shouted. "Jasper winked at me when he was standing behind La Rue and Braddock." He rushed to the master's chart room and snatched a chart and spread it on the dropdown table. Abe and Luigi followed him with the items from the dispatch pouch. "If I am not in error, Rum Cay is an island north of here, in the Bahamas." His eyes moved, immediately to the lower Bahamas. "There it is." His forefinger punched the chart right under the island."

Abe set the *Hawk's* logbook on the edge of the chart. "But what does it mean, captain?"

Nate glanced to the logbook and back to Rum Cay on the chart. "Jasper is telling us the *Hawk* is headed for Rum Cay." Abe and Luigi looked down at the chart, then over to the *Hawk's* logbook, then to Nate. Seeing the questions in their faces, he continued his speculation. "He must have overheard La Rue say he was taking the ship there." Moving the logbook off the chart he scanned the islands around Rum Cay. "Look." He called for their attention as he ran his finger at the surrounding islands. "La Rue has chosen a place right in the center of British trade in the Bahamas." He moved his finger in a clockwise circle around Rum Cay as he called out the names of the British settlements. "Cockburn Town in the north on San Salvadore." His finger began the clockwise arc. "Georgetown on Great Exuma, and over here to the southeast is Clarence Town on Long Island, and finally Colonel Hill to the South on Crooked Island." Standing up he looked to the men for concurrence. "You see, he is right in the middle of his prey, free to attack any British shipping which comes along."

"I agree with you Captain." Captain Nobbs and Lieutenant MacKensie had come to the chart table to see what the commotion was and heed Nate's analysis of Jasper's message. "We will need a plan as La Rue will be able to see any approaching ship for miles."

"I agree, Captain Nobbs. How long will it take for the *Drake* to raise Rum Cay?"

"I would say four, perhaps five days." Simon glanced up to see the sails drawing a good breeze. "That is if the wind stays with us."

"Good." Nate leaned over to study the chart. "That gives us time to devise a plan."

*****

Nathan Beauchamp peered forward from the *Drake's* forecastle. His eyes were on the horizon but his thoughts entrenched on the distant Rum Cay and the man who had taken his ship. His subconscious mind recorded the men below decks singing Christmas hymns. A light rain blew from aft, gathered on his bicorn hat then dribbled on his hand. He clutched the starboard bulwark unaware of the rain.

The watch officers tended their duties from the quarterdeck. Captain Nobbs read the slate then returned it to the binnacle. He saw Lieutenant Levy leaning on his cabin skylight and followed Levy's stare. His friend and former superior officer stared at the horizon from the ship's bow. Simon moved to Levy's side. "Your captain is a determined man."

Shell Levy glanced at Captain Nobbs then forward again to his captain. "He has to be, Captain." He watched a group of the *Hawk's* seamen timidly easing up the deck to their captain. "He does not relish explaining to the Admiralty how he lost his ship to a Frenchman and a group of Irish Rebels." Both officers walked to the quarterdeck rail to better see what the seamen were about.

Nate felt a presence behind him as he awoke from his trance like thought of Louis La Rue and turned to a group of smiling faces. "Mr. Hall." He nodded to the leader of the group. "Merry Christmas, men."

"Merry Christmas, sir," they replied in unison.

He and the group of *Hawk's* seamen stood staring at each other for a few seconds. "Is there something I can do for you men?" Nate broke the silence.

"Aye, sir." Hall stepped forward then looked back and waved the tall Moroccan, Akil Tocoma, forward.

Nate smiled to himself when he thought of how midshipmen had named the big man Sinbad. Even in British seaman's clothing he was an imposing figure that, with a little imagination, one could see the hero of the Arabian Knights.

Sinbad held out a small piece of wood for his captain.

"What is this Mr. Tocoma?" Nate asked.

Sinbad looked back to Mr. Hall, who stepped forward and pointed to the carving on the surface of wood. "It's jest kinda like a Christmas present from the *Hawks*, sir."

"Why, thank you, men." Nate saw a large, blunt bowed ship carved into the wood.

"It's the *Hawk*, sir" Hall volunteered.

"I see it is and a very well done likeness. I appreciate it very much." Nate was touched by the men's gift.

Hall stuck his thumb in the Moroccan's midsection. "Sinbad, er that is Mr. Tocoma carved it from a piece of wood he found on Fiddler's Island."

"A very artful carving indeed." He blinked his eyes to fight back a tear. "I wish I had something to give you men in return."

"You've already given us so much, sir." Hall looked back at the seamen who were nodding their heads and smiled at the captain. "You kept us work'n together on that island so's we could survive and now you're leading us ta gets our ship back."

Nate reached over and patted Hall's shoulder, then addressed the men. "I thank you, each and every one, and together we will do our best to retake the *Hawk* and get on with our mission in Florida."

Levy spoke to no one in particular. "That young man seems to instill loyalty in those around him."

Simon cut his eyes over to Shell Levy. "You don't have to tell me, Mr. Levy." Smiling slyly, he said, "He is a good man and fine officer." He adjusted his sword belt, then watched Nate react with his men on the forecastle. "Sometime remind me to tell you about the *Dart*, the *Valliant* and the *Falcon's* cruise last spring."

Shell glanced to the chuckle coming from behind him and saw Duncan MacKensie nodding his head.

*****

Lieutenant Howard Foster leaned over the starboard bulwark watching the flying fish jumping past the *Drake's* bow. The wing like fish leaped several feet out of the water, dove under for mere seconds before leaping into the still morning air, then hit the water again. Foster followed the path of the fish as they raced past the slow moving vessel. They resembled skipping stones on a millpond. A millpond is what the sea reminded him of this particular morning. He glanced at a movement in the water to the side of the ship, then smiled, as a mother porpoise and her calf mirrored the course of the *Drake*.

"Deck!" The lookout screamed from his perch atop the fore topgallant yard.

Foster shielded his eyes from the rising sun and gazed aloft to Timothy Leach, one of the few Irishman who had chosen to remain loyal to his King.

"What is it, Mr. Leach?" Lieutenant Foster answered as officer of the watch.

Leach pointed his slender long arm to a spot in the water off the larboard bow as he continued. "Wreckage, Mr. Foster, plenty of it and that's fer sure," he cried.

Foster immediately turned to the *Drake's* bosun. "Mr. Bateman, I'll have a boat placed over the side with a dependable crew to investigate," he called to the *Drake's* senior midshipman who clung to the mainmast larboard shrouds with his neck stretch out to see the wreckage. "Mr. Brett!" he yelled. "Inform Captain Nobbs and Captain Beauchamp, if you please."

Seventeen year old, Patrick Brett jumped to the deck and sped down the aft hatch to disrupt the senior officer's morning meeting. "Aye, aye, sir," he called, doffing his hat as he slipped down the hatch just below Lieutenant Foster's feet.

Foster's eye followed the longboat as it lifted above its cradle and swung out over the water, then was lowered till the taunt lines relaxed and the boat drifted back against the slow moving hull.

Captain Simon Nobbs, followed by The *Hawk's,* Captain Beauchamp, rushed on deck and watched the seamen follow Bosun Bateman into the longboat. "What is this about, Mr. Foster?"

"Sir looks like ship wreckage afloat off the larboard bow." Foster informed the *Drake's* captain.

Bosun Bateman called up from the waiting longboat. "Looks real nasty, Captain, some of the flotsam is smoldering."

"Very well bosun, shove off and have a look around." Simon tapped Nate. "We might as well take a glass to the forecastle to see what we can find from there."

Midshipman Brett eagerly fetched a glass from the binnacle and carried it to Captain Nobbs.

The officers moved forward to the forecastle with young Midshipman Brett following close behind. Nate glanced back at the smiling young man. "Come along Mr. Brett, you may see something this morning that seamen fear most."

"Fear, sir?" the lad anxiously asked.

Nate nodded. "Fire, Mr. Brett, be it an accident or an act of war."

"How is that, sir?" Brett dodged two swinging lanyards. "Perkins, secure these shroud lanyards, and be quick about it." He sped up to catch the two senior officers, then stopped to grin back at Perkins. "If you please."

Nate nodded to the lad as he instructed the seaman. "Simon, that lad has the make'ns of a fine sea officer."

"Aye, that he does," Simon watched the young man for a few moments then handed Nate the telescope. "His older brother has the brig *Speedy*, father is a captain and his grandfather a commodore." Simon watched Nate adjust the glass into focus. "As you can see, Mr. Brett comes from a seafaring family."

"Look at this, Simon." Beauchamp passed the glass to Captain Nobbs. "I think we have a survivor."

*****

Bosun Bateman pulled the longboat's tiller into his stocky body and held it as the boat moved slowly to the starboard to move through larger pieces of the wreckage. Oarsmen used their oars to shove the drifting flotsam aside to permit them to row further into the debris.

"Listen, lads." Bateman cocked his ear. The burning wood made a sizzling sound as it sank lower into the water. "There! Hear that?" he asked the crew.

"Sounds like a puppy whimpering," declared Topman Jack Rhome.

"Jack, ye been ta sea too long," Toby Cates laughed. "More like o'l Neptune com'n ta takes us away." Toby let loose with a horselaugh to match his long narrow face.

"Quiet! You two," belched the bosun. "Listen!" The smoke from a large section of ship blew over the boat and stung his eyes. He squeezed his eyes into tiny slits and peered ahead. A puff of morning wind parted the smoke and Bateman locked eyes with a man in ragged clothing tied to a cross, fabricated from broken ship's spars. The man's soot smudged face concealed his nationality. His eyes cried pain and when he opened his mouth to cry out, blood ran down his face trailing over his short beard. He emitted the most pitiful whimpering sound and then he dropped his head to his chest. It was then that Bateman noted the man's arms were tied on the crossed spars like a crucifix. Emilio Ortega dropped his oar and made the sign of the cross.

*****

Nate watched through the doorway of his cabin where the man laid on his cot. The *Dart's* surgeon, Gerald O'Dell, bathed the man's face with a cloth dipped in cool water. "Who is he, Mr. O'Dell?

The surgeon shook his head. "He is in a lot of pain, captain," he replied as he pulled what was remaining of the man's shirt from his blistered skin. "I have nothing to give him except rum and it burns what is remaining of his tongue." The man rolled his pleading eyes toward Nate.

"They cut out his tongue?" Nate stepped into the cabin to stand next to the surgeon and over the man. "How can he tell us who did this?"

Surgeon O'Dell slowly shook his head. "I am afraid he cannot tell you who his tormentors were, Captain."

The man clutched Nate's arm then tried to speak.

Beauchamp flinched at the man's grip. "What kind of man could do this to another?"

The man glanced to the cabin bulkhead, then painfully raised his hand and pointed to Sinbad's carving of the *Hawk*.

"A ship like this?" Nate asked the man as he removed the carving and held it for the man to see.

The man grasped the carved wood from Nate's hands and then ran his fingers over the carved words below the ship. *H.M.S. HAWK*. He looked into Nate's eye.

"The *Hawk* did this?" Nate asked.

The man nodded, as much as his injuries permitted, then drew a deep breath. His hands slid from the carving and drooped over the side of the cot and his eyes stared to the overhead. Nate looked to the surgeon.

O'Dell nodded. "He will suffer no more."

*****

Captain Beauchamp slowly moved up the ladder to the quarterdeck and stood at the leeward rail staring into the dark.

"Captain Beauchamp," Simon called as he crossed the deck. "How is he?"

Nate continued to stare seaward. "He is dead, Simon."

"Poor wretch," Simon replied as he joined Nate at the rail. "Did you learn who attacked his ship?"

"The *Hawk*." Nate studied his friend's face. "Simon, I feel responsible for the death of those men and any others La Rue sends to their death with the *Hawk*."

"You cannot hold yourself responsible for their deaths." Simon stated, attempting to cheer him up.

"It is my ship." Nate turned and walked aft. "I all but gave the ship to La Rue." Simon made to interrupt him but Nate cut him off and continued. "I am responsible for what ships he has destroyed and those he will destroy, until I stop him."

Simon took Nate's elbow and guided him to the quarterdeck ladder. "Then we had better devise a plan to take the *Hawk*, my friend."

*****

The plan was in play. The *Dart* took the short passage to the southern waters of the Virgin Islands to patrol the waters normally thick with traders between French St. Martin and Danish St. Croix to search for a French built vessel suitable to fulfill their plan.

It was a stroke of luck that, so soon after dipping south of the Virgins, events would turn to their favor.

Captain Nobbs invited his first officer, Mr. MacKensie, his midshipman, Mr. Brett, along with Captain Beauchamp and his first officer, Mr. Kent, to dine in his cabin. Crowded as they were in the tiny cabin, all were in good spirits now that a plan had been detailed to the officers.

Kersey, Captain Nobbs cabin servant, along with two assistants pressed for the occasion, brought in the first serving. With the captain's cabin full of officers around a table borrowed from the gunroom, Kersey needed to step only four feet from his pantry with the first serving, a hearty local turtle soup. With no space to navigate around the table in the crowded cabin, Kersey sat two steaming hot bowls on the table to be passed around. His assistants followed with additional bowls to be passed in the same manner. Then Kersey ushered the two assistants back to the pantry to prepare the main course of lobster with sides of butter, lemon, and wine sauce for serving.

Abe Kent held the bowl to his face and drank in the spicy aroma of the turtle soup. "I don't think I have smelled anything this fragrant for quite some time."

Captain Nobbs swallowed his first taste of turtle soup. "It is a dish of Trinidad. The home of my cook." He dove his spoon deep into the bowl and pulled out a large piece of turtle meat. "They use many different spices in their cooking." His eyes watered from the hot pepper seasoning. "Too spicy for some." He grinned at his guest as he chewed the meat and wiped the tears from his eyes.

Duncan MacKensie politely nudged his bowl to the center of the table. "Beg pardon, Simon, I know you love this local spicy food but I prefer to wait for the lobster."

Beauchamp glanced at Simon. "Simon, how long have you been at sea?"

Simon finished chewing the turtle meat and smiled. "You wonder how we eat so well after so many weeks at sea." He wiped the dribble of juice from his chin. "We bought this, the lobster and some fish, from a fishing drogue off Tortola." He replied and drove his spoon in the soup once more. "We ate the fish that night but kept the turtle alive in the manger and the lobster in an old water keg till this morning," Smiling around the table as he bragged. "If nothing else, we eat well on the *Drake*."

Nate stirred his bowl sending the spicy fragrance upward. "It does smell wonderful." Then slipped the very tip of the spoon between his lips and let the broth dribble across his tongue. "Mmm." He murmured, taking the entire contents of the spoon for a better taste. "This is very..." He was cut short by a knock on the cabin door.

"Yes!" Simon called to the closed door.

The door creaked open and a short balding seaman poked his head in the door. He clutched his watch cap in his callused hands and wrinkled his nose smelling the turtle soup.

"What is it, Chaney?" Captain Nobbs demanded.

"Sir, Mr. Shepard, sends 'is compliments and thar be a sail afore da bow."

"Thank you, Chaney, please convey to Mr. Shepard that I will be on deck shortly."

Seaman Chaney raised his neck to peek at the food on the officer's table.

"That will be all, Chaney," he said, dismissing the seaman.

The seaman blushed at being caught and eased out the door to deliver the captain's message.

"Gentlemen, let us finish this fine turtle soup and go topside to take a look." Simon tipped his bowl up and drained its remaining broth.

Duncan emitted a low moan, glanced to the pantry and the waiting lobster, then took a ship's biscuit and dipped it in the large bowl of mayonnaise as his stomach growled.

*****

Nathan Beauchamp took the offered glass from Lieutenant Howard Foster. "Looks like a local lugger, sir."

Nate lifted the telescope and adjusted it to bring the craft close enough to see the details. The vessel sat deep in the water and sailed slowly. She labored to make way with her heavy cargo. "A chasse-maree', Mr. Foster."

Howard Foster stared forward for a short time, studying the ship. "I thought for sure she to be a lugger, sir."

"There is a slight difference, Mr. Foster," he said, handed the glass back to the young lieutenant and pointed to the slow moving ship. "She has two masts instead of the three of English luggers. See her stern is somewhat rounded, a clear sign of a French chasse-maree, she has no bowsprit and has three stay sails," he instructed as he placed his hand on the lieutenant's shoulder turning the officer slightly, then ran his hand up and down, simulating the backwards slant of the mainmast. "See the slope of the mainmast? It is farther to the back than our luggers."

"Why does she not run, sir? Surely she can see we are a British war ship." Foster asked.

"See how low she sits in the water?" Captain Beauchamp indicated where the ship's waterline should be but was below the water. "She is most likely sailing as fast as she can." Beauchamp directed Foster to the ship's sails. Her topgallant sails are full, she is struggling to escape but is most likely sailing as fast as she can go with that cargo." He turned at the sound of *Drake's* gun crew running out the bowchaser. "That fellow's greed will be his undoing." Covering his ears and nudged the lieutenant to do the same.

The larboard bowchaser erupted and sent a four-pound ball across the chasse-maree's bow. The Frenchmen rushed to drop her sails as she slowed to a stop and rocked in the rollers.

Nate watched the *Drake's* longboat lifted from her storage rack and dropped slowly alongside. The boarding party drew weapons and climbed over the side to lower themselves to the boat. Nate glanced aft to meet Simon's eyes.

"Be my guest, Captain Beauchamp." He nodded to the boarding party waiting in the longboat.

Nate nodded his thanks to the *Drake's* captain. "Mr. Levy, on me, if you please."

The *Hawk's* seasoned new second officer swung his leg over the bulwark, and climbed down the rope ladder, answering as he lowered himself to the longboat. "Aye, aye, sir."

Beauchamp climbed down the ladder and took his seat in the longboat. "Mr. Bateman, if you please." Nate called for the *Drake's* bosun to shove off for the chasse-maree.

The *Drake's* boarding party pulled hard for the chasse-maree, no doubt with prize money on their minds. As the longboat closed with the ship, Nate studied her in detail. She was a very plain working ship, with little or no frills. He name plate said she was the *Voyageur Allegre* home ported in Marigot, French St. Martin. No doubt she was familiar in these trade route waters between St. Martin and St. Croix.

The ship's rigging blocks clanged against the mast and spars as she rolled in the gentle seas. The boarding party threw a painter to the deck for the Frenchmen to tie the longboat to the ship's side. Nate followed the armed *Drake's* seamen up the side to the deck to find the *Voyageur Allegre's* crew consisted of two French officers and six crewmen of mixed African and French blood. The civilian ship's master approached Beauchamp offering his sword. Nate took the sword passing it to Bosun Bateman. "I will have your manifest now, captain."

The French captain shrugged his shoulders, indicating his inability to comprehend English.

Lieutenant Levy translated Captain Beauchamp's demand for the ship's papers.

The chasse-maree's captain motioned his clerk forward and took the manifest from him, glanced at the document, and passed it to Captain Beauchamp.

"Mr. Levy, I believe your papers said you have a command of written French as well." Beauchamp reached the papers to Lieutenant Levy. "I can read French, however it takes me a while to struggle through it." He grinned.

"Yes, sir." Shell Levy took the papers and immediately scanned the documents. Halfway through the papers, Shell glanced to his captain. "French shot and Danish powder, sir."

Nate glanced around the deck. "That explains why she sits so low in the water." He turned to the chasse-maree's captain. "Please tell the captain we must take his ship."

Lieutenant Levy commenced translating Beauchamp's orders to the Frenchman.

Captain Beauchamp continued. "He and his men can assist us in dropping the shot over the side, in which case they will be placed ashore on a neutral island." He walked down the line of French prisoners. "Should they not assist us they will be sent to the *Drake* where they will spend the remainder of our mission in the cable tier, in irons." He walked back past the line of prisoners to arrive at the French Captain as Mr. Levy completed his translation of his message to the Frenchman.

The French captain's eyes showed his understanding of the consequence of not assisting the British. He glanced to his men who jabbered their pleas to accept the British captain's generous offer to place them ashore for assisting with dumping the French shot over the side. Grinning, he turned to face Beauchamp. "Oui, monsieur." He motioned for his men to open the hatches.

Nate nodded to the Frenchman to commence dumping the shot over the side. "Bosun Bateman, return to the *Drake* and send the *Hawk's* men over, if you please." He walked the bosun to the ship's side. "Tell Captain Nobbs as soon as we have this shot over the side, we will get under way and execute our plan to sail to the Bahamas."

Nate stared across the open water between the *Drake* and the *Voyageur Allegre.* He smiled, if his French was correct, *Voyageur Allegre* meant, " Lively Voyage". *We shall see how lively this voyage will be.* And turned his head at the splash of the first canon ball over the side.

Chapter Nine

Rum Cay

The Voyageur Allegre followed in *Drake's* wake from the southern waters of the Virgin Islands to the center islands of the Bahamas Colony. Her French and mulatto crew had long been rowed ashore on a section of Haiti's uninhabited north coast as promised. The chasse-maree's prize master, Lieutenant Shell Levy, strained his eyes in the dark night to keep station on the *Dart*.

"Mr. Levy, I believe the *Dart* is reducing sail." John Wright, former powder monkey and now prize crewmember, called from the *Voyageur Allegre's* bow.

The middle aged lieutenant moved forward as quietly in his sea boots as the seamen moved about the deck in bare feet. He had already reminded the men that sound carries far over open water and the Frenchman may have scout vessels patrolling in the darkness to protect from just such an attack as Captains

Beauchamp and Nobbs had planned. Levy stared towards the *Dart* with the night glass on loan to him from Lieutenant MacKensie. "You have good eyes, Mr. Wright." He rubbed the lad's sandy blond hair in approval. "We will make a seaman of you yet."

The young boy grinned at the compliment as they both silently slipped aft where Mr. Levy whispered the order to reduce sail then told quartermasters mate Iodice to steer the chasse-maree to the brig's side.

"Mr. McClain, have the cutter readied, if you please." Levy ordered the *Hawk's* master to commence with the first phase of the plan.

"Aye, sir." McClain nodded to Topman Bobby Mantell to apply the galley's slush to the blocks that would lift the scout cutter over the side. The greasy slush had been scooped from the top of the cooking kettles these last few days and was used to lubricate the normally squeaky blocks. Mantell and his assistant completed lubricating the two blocks then stood aside as idlers pulled the ropes lifting the *Drake's* cutter from the chasse-maree's deck.

"Wait," whispered Andreas Pappas, the *Hawk's* carpenter. He leaned over and lifted the small mast and sail. Sail maker, Alberto Trifiro grabbed the far end, and then together they placed them aboard the cutter. Mr. Pappas waved upward, signaling the idlers to continue lifting the boat over the side. "Is a better dis a way." He grinned.

"I agree, Mr. Pappas." Levy glanced to the larboard rail, then watched Captain

Beauchamp and Major Scarlet climb over the rail from the *Dart's* longboat. They were followed by four hand-chosen men from the crews of the *Hawk* and *Dart*.

"Evening, Mr. Levy." Captain Beauchamp and Major Scarlet wore lightweight, dark clothing, suitable for those not wishing to be seen on a covert scouting mission. "Is the cutter about ready?"

"Aye, sir. She is just now in the water and her sail has been darkened as you ordered." Lieutenant Levy guided the two officers to the rail overlooking where the cutter, secured by a long painter, rode beside the chasse-maree.

"Good work, Mr. levy." Nate squeezed Levy's arm. "I would like to borrow Mr. Mantell for his good eyes, if you can spare him."

"By all means, sir." Shell Levy motioned for seaman Mantell to board the cutter. "Sir, might I recommend you take Mr. Wright." He nodded, pointing out the tiny lad. "He is ready to step up from powder monkey and commence training for a more seaman like role."

Nate beckoned to the lad. "How old are you, Mr. Wright?"

"Twelve years old, sir," he nervously answered, then added, "Last month, sir."

Nate grinned at the nervous lad. "I was about your age when I went on my first mission." He rubbed the boy's hair then motioned to the cutter. "Very well, Mr. Wright, in the cutter with you." He watched the youngster puff up his chest as he brazenly strode over to the rail and lowered himself down to the cutter. "Where is the boy from?"

Mr. McClain approached Captain Beauchamp and Mr. Levy. "He just showed up one day at the ship yard and sort of adopted us. Said he ran away from an orphanage." McClain grinned. "So we had him make his mark in the roster book."

"We shall see how he does and perhaps we can accommodate some future training for him." Beauchamp moved from the boy to his orders for Mr. Levy. "After we depart, you and the *Dart* will withdraw to just over the horizon." Glancing to the men waiting in the cutter then back to Lieutenant Levy, he continued, "Shell, if we do not return by this time tomorrow night, you will be under Captain Nobbs orders."

"I'll not worry, sir. You will return safely and we will be here waiting for you," Shell Levy reassured Captain Beauchamp.

Nate grinned and shook Shell's offered hand, checked his pocket timepiece to find it ten in the evening. He glanced at the darkened horizon to assure night cloaked the scouting mission then climbed down into the cutter. "Shove off, Mr. Bateman."

*****

The past few weeks of working together on the decks and rigging of the *Drake* gave the mixed boat crew the ability to function as a practiced and unified team. Britons and foreign nationals worked in the moonless night, shoulder to shoulder, lifting the mast and setting the small sail. Wind puffed the sail sending the boom to its starboard limit and pushed the cutter through the darkness on their mission toward Rum Cay.

Minutes seemed like hours as the small cutter sped in the direction of the island suspected to be the location of Louis La Rue and the ship he had stolen from Nathan Beauchamp. Sure-eyed Bobby Mantell sat in the bow of the *Drake's* cutter, staring at the horizon before him. His eyes searched for the faintest of lights that might reveal the hiding place where La Rue and the *Hawk* lay waiting to pounce on unsuspecting British merchant ships and local traders. The sound of small waves lapped at the sides of the cutter as it sped along a predetermined mark of the compass.

Nate stared forward in the darkness covering the cutter. His eyes, having adjusted to the night, picked out individual members of the crew. Most sat leaning against the boat's sides, resting for when their strength would be required to row the small craft. Little John Wright sat just aft of Mr. Mantell, he clutched the mast forward shrouds with one hand. He too scanned the horizon for any sign of light. The blowing wind that pushed the cutter blew his long blond hair forward, over his shoulders and down his chest. The damp air pushed into his face and the cutter moved forward. He blinked his watering eyes and concentrated on his self appointed mission of being the first to find the enemy.

"I smells land." Seaman Jack Rhome stirred from his light sleep. He sat upright, leaned his nose forward and sniffed.

"You don't smell noth'n, Jack," Toby Cates whispered from across the cutter's girth. "Cept may'bee yor upper lip." Toby glanced around at the grinning faces nearest him. "Most likely you ain't washed it in a fortnight." Quartermaster's mate Iodice chuckled at Toby's comment and the way Jack and Toby were always having a go with each other.

"Quiet!" Bosun Bateman chastised the noisy men before the captain could. "I smells rotten'n mangroves." He nodded his head to Nate. "And that's fer sure."

"Might be very close to the island now." Beauchamp arched his neck upward to look over the heads of the now awake men. Pitch-blackness stared back at him. He retracted his neck and offered the tiller. "Take the tiller for a spell, Mr. Bateman, if you please." Nate went over the *Drake's* chart in his mind. "With the course we set from the chasse-maree, we should first make Junkanoo Rock," he recalled as he mentally checked the chart once again. "From there we will steer North, Mr. Bateman. Keep out to sea and away from the coral reefs or we'll be done for." Beauchamp stretched his legs and rubbed a cramp from his calf. "Sail along the North coast till we sight lights, then we will have the sail off her and row the remainder of the way."

Jack Rhome moaned at the thought of a long row. "They may see the sail, Mr. Rhome. We can't give ourselves away before we get a good look, now can we?" Nate explained to the seaman.

"No, sir, your honor." Jack rubbed his upper arm. "Its just I could row so much better when I were a young lad. He pulled on his fingers and stretched them backwards. "That were afore I got the a'flictions in me bones."

Toby Cates nudged the Italian, Iodice, then leaned over so Rhome could better hear him. "You ain't never been young, you o'l goat."

"Why, I have so, Toby Cates, you lubber," Jack shot back at his friend. "I remembers once when I were on the..." Jack was cut of from Mr. Mantell.

"Light to the larboard, sir," Mantell called softly.

Nate slipped through the men as they drew up their feet to give him passage to the bow. "Where away, Mr. Mantell?"

Bobby Mantell pointed. Nate adjusted his eyes to the darkness at the end of Mantell's hand. He studied the gloom for several seconds before he saw the flickering light. "House, most likely. These people live like hermits scattered among these islands." He heard little John Wright exhale a breath of disappointment behind him. "Not to worry, Mr. Wright, that is not the light we seek." He turned to go to his seat at the tiller and patted the lad on the head as he passed. "We still have a long way to go,

Mr. Wright. You still may be the first to sight the enemy."

The cutter skirted the coral reefs as she sailed westward for the next two hours. Mr. Bateman issued water and biscuit to the men at two bells. When they finished their Spartan meal Nate nodded to the bosun to take the sail down. The remainder of the way would be under manpower.

*****

Bosun Bateman gazed larboard from his seat at the tiller. His thoughts of his previous visit to the island stirred his mind. "Desolate place, this island."

"What was that, bosun?" Nate asked.

"This island is a desolate place," he replied as he pulled his pipe from his coat pocket and wedged it in between his old yellowed teeth. "I were here a few months ago and there ain't much of anything here. Flat land with a few rolling hills, low brush and a few trees, noth'n most people would want." Realizing he could not light the pipe, he stuffed it back in his pocket.

"Just what a rogue like La Rue would want." Nate wiped the salt spray from his face. "No one to bother him and just a few miles from the other island shipping lanes."

Both Nate and Bosun Bateman watched the men's easy pace at the oars. Young Jack Wright shivered from the morning dampness. Bobby Mantell pulled the lad next to him and draped the left side of his coat over his shoulders. They watched the darkness for lights together.

The bosun held the tiller with his elbow and fidgeted with his small tobacco sack. A piece of the plug fell out of the bag and into the cutters bilge. Major Scarlet reached between the bilge slats and fished it out then handed it to the bosun. "Thankee kindly, Major." Bateman turned it over, looking for evidence of damage, then wiped it on his trousers, popped it in his mouth and clamped his teeth down.

The major and Captain Beauchamp watched Bateman chew his tobacco like a cow chewing a cud.

"That island weren't always called Rum Cay," Bateman quibbled. Nate and Ronald Scarlet smiled as Bateman shifted attention away from his tobacco chewing. Bateman leaned slightly and spit tobacco juice down wind. "That Columbee feller found it first and named it Santa Maria de la Conception over three hundred years ago." Nate and the major watched as they listened to the old bosun. Bateman leaned and spit again then wiped his mouth with his sleeve. "A Yankee ship head'n home with a hold full of Jamakee rum ran aground and sunk on one of the reefs over there." He pointed into the darkness, toward the island. "I hear"d they was scoop'n up bottles of rum around this island fer years." Bosun Bateman spit the tobacco plug over the side then picked a piece of leaf from between his teeth, tried to examine it in the dark, then flicked it down wind. "Recon that's how it got the name Rum Cay."

"That is very interesting, boson, but sure ya don't hold with such truck?" Jack Rhome called over his shoulder as he drove his oar deep into the water and pulled it to him.

"I ain't barter'n no story," Bateman puffed up his chest with indignation. "It's mor-n-likely fact, Jack Rhome."

Captain Beauchamp listened more than watched the bosun and Jack Rhome bicker in their unnatural whispering voices. His eyes adjusted so well to the dark, he considered for a moment that he might have the eyes of a cat. He sensed movement in the bow and glanced up to see Mantell nudge the sleepy John Wright to look off the cutter's larboard bow. "Lights, sir!" The boy jumped up excitedly pointing to the distant Flamingo Bay. "Many lights, sir!"

"Not so loud, lad." Mantell pulled the boy back down to his previous crouching position. The oarsmen craned their necks around to see the lights.

"Never you mind what's up forward, just keep rowing, lads." The bosun ordered.

Nate again moved forward between the oarsmen and crouched in the bow with Mantell and the boy. "Take us one hundred yards to larboard then lay too, Mr. Bateman.

"Aye, sir." He gave the order to the oarsmen and added, "Now put yer backs into it lads."

*****

The cutter gently rolled in the early morning swells while Nate and Major Scarlet studied the ships anchored in the bay. "That's the *Hawk*, alright, I'd know her Old Dutch hull anywhere." Nate grinned, his hunch was correct. "Looks like two ships inboard of her." He lifted his night glass and adjusted it to bring it into focus, starring a few moments while he grew accustomed to seeing the ships upside down. *If science can make a telescope to see in the dark, why can't they make one that displays everything up right?*

"What do you make of them, Captain Beauchamp?" Major Scarlet stuck his head so close to Nate that he handed the eager major the glass.

"Looks to be a fat merchantman closest to the shore, the middle ship looks to be some type of gun ketch, *Hawk* is anchored with the other two tied to her." Nate gave his summation of the situation.

Major Scarlet lowered the glass and stared at Nate. "The pirate was a top-sail gun ketch, was she not?"

"Yes, that makes sense." Beauchamp stared at the anchored ships "Looks like Black Caser and La Rue." He stopped speaking for a moment, then continued, "The other ship must be either Irish Rebels or a captured merchantman." Nate started aft toward tiller. "No matter, there are too many for us to handle." Sitting next to the bosun he continued. "Mr. Bateman, take us two hundred yards straight out to sea. It should be far enough in this darkness to get the sail back on her, then we can turn her head towards the *Dart* and the chase-maree.

"Thank God fer small favors." Mumbled Jack Rhome.

"What was that you said, Rhome?" Bateman demanded.

"Noth'n, bosun, I were just thank'n God that I were on this here cutter when them scurvy Frenchies was found." Jack bared his gap tooth grin at Bosun Bateman.

Bosun Bateman grinned at the cranky oarsman. "Jack, one o' these days that sour mouth of yourn is gonna get you flogged."

*****

It had taken the *Drake's* cutter longer to return to the rendezvous with the *Drake* and *Voyageur Allegre* than planned. A strong southerly wind caused them to fight headlong winds most of the way. Continuous tacking added hours to their return journey.

The cutter had long been returned to her storage rack on the *Drake's* deck and her crew well fed and rested. Below deck the officers and warrants sat quietly around the long oak table in the gunroom listening to Captain Beauchamp's briefing on the plan to attack the three ships at anchor in Flamingo Bay.

"Gentlemen, The *Dart* and the *Voyageur Allegre* cannot take on the guns of those three ships on the open sea." Nate shifted in his seat at the head of the table. "If that were the case we could just wait till they come out of the bay and have a go at them broadside to broadside but the *Hawk's* guns alone could sink both our ships." He sipped the rum so graciously provided by the gunroom's officers then continued. "No, we must fool the Frenchman into thinking the chase-maree is fleeing from a British man of war." Nate glanced up to the overhead and cocked his ear at the hammering on the *Drake's* main deck then turned to Simon. "Captain Nobbs, would you care to brief the plan?"

"Thank you, Captain Beauchamp." Nobbs slid back the small bench he sat on and stood to be better heard in the crowded cabin. "Gentlemen, we intend to fill the chase-maree with as many armed men as she can hold. You will have to withstand the heat under a canvas but the reward in prize money should make it bearable for you." The mention of prize money gathered everyone's attention. Simon now faced an attentive audience of grinning officers and warrants. "I will keep only enough men to sail the ship and man the bow chasers." He set three small pieces of wood, with slender pegs for mast, beside each other then placed two more pieces of wood on the table, one behind the other. "These three are the *Hawk*, *Royalist* and the merchantman, tied abreast." Nobbs moved the remaining two pieces of wood, one in each hand, towards the three pieces of wood representing the enemy. "The *Dart* will pursue the chase-maree, firing her bow chasers. The Frenchman will believe one of his countrymen to be fleeing from a British brig." He slid the chase-maree along side of the *Hawk*. "Hopefully the chase-maree will block the *Hawk's* guns from firing on the *Drake* while our boarders take the advantage of surprising the Frenchmen and his Irish Rebels."

"Sir." Lieutenant Foster raised his hand.

"Yes, Mr. Foster." Simon nodded for Foster to proceed with his question.

"Will not the tarpaulin look suspicious to the Frenchman?" Foster askcd.

Captain Nobbs' hands began cutting squares and curves in the air above the table. "As we speak." He pointed to the deck above. "Mr. Papas and his mates are constructing frames that when covered with canvas will appear to be crates and barrels draped with canvas to protect them from the elements."

"I see, sir." Foster nodded his concurrence of the ruse.

"Captain Beauchamp, Sir." Ezra McClain stood to address the *Hawk's* Captain. "Won't La Rue think it strange a French trader being chased in British waters?" The *Hawk's* master sat down and glanced around the table at the nodding heads.

"Good point, Mr. McClain." Nate stroked his ear, searching for the correct words. "Our plan depends largely on La Rue seeing what he wants to see. Greed will drive him to wait for the *Drake* to come into range of *Hawk's* guns." He grinned around the table as he laid his theory before the officers and warrants. "He will think himself quite the hero, saving a French merchantman and destroying or taking a British ship-of-war."

Duncan MacKensie stared straight ahead, running his hand up and down his empty glass then turned to Nate. "Captain, for our sake, I hope this La Rue fellow reacts as you expect."

"I believe he is greedy and overly confident." Nate Beauchamp stood, indicating an end to the briefing. "Those are usually predictable traits, Mr. MacKensie, I believe we have the upper hand."

*****

Louis La Rue, captain in the French Republican Navy and now master of the *Hawk*, rose from the head of the long oak dinning table in the *Hawk's* great cabin. He tapped his spoon on the edge of his glass. His guests ceased talking and waited for La Rue to speak. La Rue raised the glass to Thomas Hayes at the far end of the table, then dipped it to the pirate Black Caesar. "Monsieur gentlemen." He nodded to Barbara and Christina Hayes. "And gracious ladies, may I propose a toast to the success of our venture, the freedom of Ireland and the health of Napoleon, Emperor of France."

Thomas and Black Caesar rose and held their glasses up to La Rue. Thomas spoke first. "Here, here!" Thomas and La Rue raised their glasses to their lips.

"Wait!" Black Caesar raised a protest. La Rue and Thomas stopped with their glasses to their lips and questioningly rolled their eyes to the pirate. "What about the gentlemen of my profession?" The intoxicated Black Caesar slurred.

La Rue lowered his glass. "Quite right you are Monsieur Caesar, without your discovery of the *San Pedro* and your willingness to include us in your salvage venture, we would not be so close to funding weapons for our Irish friends." As he raised his glass, he continued, "To the gentlemen in the piracy profession." The glasses of French Champagne were downed, then Thomas and Caesar took their seats, while La Rue remained standing. "May you always be on our side." He smiled and then took his seat.

Caesar grabbed the champagne bottle and splashed the contents into his glass, drunkenly running the champagne over the rim and on to the white tablecloth. "A true pirate is on the side what pays 'em the most." Caesar belly laughed at his own joke.

"So I have been told, Captain Caesar." La Rue slid his glass to the side so Jasper could refill it. He cocked his ear toward the great cabin's gun port. "Did you hear a canon?" He asked no one in particular.

"More'n likely thunder." Caesar flipped his hand backwards, passing the noise as of no significance. "The British have only small sloops and cutters in these waters."

Mathew Braddock burst through the cabin door. "Louis! There is a French luger with all sail pressed run'n from a British brig."

"Perhaps you mean, chase-maree, Monsieur Braddock." Louis La Rue crossed the cabin and passed through the door Braddock had left open.

Braddock followed him on his way to the main deck. "Aye, sir, chase-maree was my mean'n, fer sure."

La Rue's dinner guest followed him up the ladder and stood behind him watching the two ships sailing towards Flamingo Bay and the *Hawk*.

La Rue called to the quarterdeck. "Run up our flag." He glanced seaward, watching the British ship fire her bow chasers, nearly missing the chase-maree's rudder. "Signal the chase-maree to run in behind the *Castle Bar*," he shouted to Jean Reule as he tied off the French flag. Reule rushed to the flag locker and pulled flags from the locker that matched La Rue's signal according to the most current French signal book.

La Rue shoved Braddock to the Irishmen watching the chase. "Have the guns loaded but do not run out till I give the order." He smiled to Thomas Hayes and his sisters. "That British fellow has taken on more than he can handle." They watched Black Caesar stagger across the deck and disappear over the side down to the *Royaliste*.

"Perhaps our pirate friend is not as brave and fierce as he would have us believe." Barbara and Christina knowingly smiled at his remark. Louis returned their smile and bowed slightly. "Perhaps you ladies would enjoy my destruction of the British brig more comfortably from the quarterdeck.

*****

Shell Levy and the two men at the chase-maree's wheel ducked as seawater splashed over them. He glanced to the chasing brig. "Captain Nobbs sent that ball a little too near for my comfort." He removed his hat and shook the water from the brim, then replaced it as he wiped his face semidry with his other hand.

"Signal from the *Hawk*, Mr. Levy," Mantell shouted from his station on the ship's bow.

Nate and Abe Kent stuck their heads out from under the canvas-covered frame, watching and listening.

"Thank you, Mr. Mantell." Shell rummaged through the papers in the black, leather bag he brought on deck from the French captain's cabin. He found what he was searching for and pulled out the French signal book. Levy laid it atop the binnacle box and leafed through the pages while he studied the flags streaming from the *Hawk's* masts through his telescope. "Just as you predicted, captain," he shouted to the two heads jutting up from under the canvas. "He has invited us to hide behind the anchored ships."

"How far are we from the *Hawk*?" Nate shouted above the sound of the *Drake's* bow chasers.

Shell peered forward. "A cable's length, no more." He motioned to the waiting seamen to trim the sails.

"Shell!" Beauchamp shouted to attract the busy second officer's attention.

Shell glanced down while taking the wheel from the quartermaster. "Sir?"

"Remember to turn the ship at the last possible moment." Nate grinned to reassure the man who now had complete control of how well the plan came off.

Shell quickly looked back to see the *Drake's* sails trimming as she turned side on as if to fire her broadside at the fleeing chase-maree. He snapped his head forward and prepared to turn the ship. The chase-maree's bowsprit seemed to almost strike the *Hawk's* stern lights but he knew he still had several yards to go. The faces of two women on the *Hawk's* quarterdeck became clear as he drew near. Behind them he recognized Captain Beauchamp's servant, Jasper, standing with a knowing smile on his dark face.

He turned the wheel with all his might, pushing the spokes as fast as his strength would allow. The chase-maree heeled over, the seamen dropped the sails and she speedily drifted along side the *Hawk*. The men ran from dropping the sail and grabbed the grappling hooks from their pre-staged locations and flung them up and over the *Hawk's* high bulwarks and pulled the two ships together.

The alarmed La Rue pulled his sword and moved back from the rail. He yelled to the men manning the canons. "Arm yourselves, it is a British trick."

The Irishmen and Frenchmen at the guns ran to the center of the *Hawk's* deck to find La Rue had never ordered the arms chest to be brought up from the armory. He had been fooled into seeing what he wanted to see. He was sure the *Hawk's* guns would destroy the British brig as he saved the French chase-maree.

The British boarders came over the *Hawk's* bulwark, yelling like savages with Captain Beauchamp in the lead. Most of the Irish and French mutineers turned and ran across the *Royaliste* to the Castle Bar, seeking safety.

Barbara and Christine drew their swords and rushed to the main deck bulwark and escape to the deck of Black Caesar's pirate ship *Royaliste.* Christina sheathed her sword, threw her legs over the bulwark and slid down to the deck. She looked up to the *Hawk* for Barbara.

Nate rushed across the *Hawk's* deck to kill the fleeing mutineer, dressed in black. He cocked his pistol and reached it out to the mutineer's head.

"No! Cap'n." Jasper pulled Beauchamp's arm and the pistol down, causing it to fire into the deck.

The captain glanced to see his servant and friend's face then back to the mutineer dressed in black. The mutineer stood facing him with his sword at the ready. With blade pressing against blade Nate looked down his opponent's blade and slowly up the mutineer's chest with his gaze stopping on the face. "Barbara!" A surprised Nate called the name of his recent desires.

Barbara smiled and parried Nate's sword, pushing it away from her torso. "How nice to see you again, Commander Beauchamp."

They crossed blades with Nate forcing her back against the bulwark. He flipped his sword upward knocking her sword to the deck, then held his blade to her chest. "Your god uncle will be disappointed to find you and your family to be Irish Rebels."

She winced as the point of his blade pierced her blouse and pricked her skin. A tiny drop of blood seeped through making a small spot on her red garment a darker hue as she forced a smile. "We do what we must to obtain freedom for our homeland."

Nate ignored the noise of battle around them. "Do you surrender?"

"Never!" The determined fire in her eyes matched the color of her billowing hair.

"Are you quite sure, Miss Hayes?" He flicked his wrist downward, cutting free the buttons of her bodice, freeing her previously constrained flesh then he instantly returned the blade to its original position above her breast.

Barbara gasped and instinctively brought her hands up to pull the bodice together. "You are no gentleman, sir."

His tone of voice deepened. "I can not afford to be a gentleman when the welfare of our British Union is at risk." He applied more pressure to the sword against her chest. "You must surrender or perish."

"Barbara, hurry." Christina called to her sister from the deck of the *Royaliste*.

Nate momentarily glanced to the sound of Christina's voice, then felt a blow to his head.

With his sight dimming, he dropped to his knees, then fell to the deck.

Barbara turned to Jasper who still held the belaying pin as he stared down at his Captain's limp body. "Thank you, Jasper." She squeezed his arm and leaped over the bulwark then raced with Christina to the *Castle Bar* as the ship pulled away, loaded with the remaining rebels and pirates.

Jasper watched the *Castle Bar* sail out of Flamingo Bay and past the *Drake,* while Captain Nobbs, with his skeleton crew, could do nothing more than fire his bow chasers at the escaping rebels. He stooped down, taking Nate's head in his lap and brushed the coal black hair from his captain's impassive face. "I sho do be mighty sorry, Cap'n."

The Irish and French still fighting dropped what weapons they had to the deck and watched their hope of escape sail towards the setting sun.

Abe Kent also watched the *Castle Bar* sailing away. He wiped the blood from his blade then ordered. "Lock these traitors below, Mr. Foster."

Duncan MacKensie pulled Abe's arm and nodded to the sound of swordplay on the quarterdeck. They rushed up the ladder to find Shell Levy and La Rue locked in desperate combat.

The two adversaries locked their swords at the hilts, then La Rue smashed his fist aside Shell's face knocking him back a step. With Levy's pressure against his sword removed, La

Rue fell forward. As Shell stumbled backwards, he swung his sword in an arc at the Frenchman, cutting deep into La Rue's side. The Frenchman grasped his side and fell to his knees.

Shell Levy recovered from his stumble and now stood towering above the wounded French officer. He dove his sword into the Frenchman's chest. La Rue fell to the deck, lying on his back with Shell's sword protruding from his chest. Shell placed his boot on La Rue's chest and yanked his sword free. "That's one Frenchman who won't be taking anymore British ships."

"The captain has been wounded." Master McClain rushed up the quarterdeck ladder, and then stopped to stare at Shell Levy standing over the dead Frenchman.

Kent and MacKensie glanced at the master, and then hurried down the ladder to see to Captain Beauchamp.

Master McClain crossed the deck, took the trancelike Lieutenant Levy by the elbow and guided him to the main deck. "Come on, Mr. Levy, it's over now, sir."

Chapter Ten

Matecombe Key

Nathan Beauchamp touched his bandage-wrapped head, then slid his hand along the bandage to the lump on the back.

Simon Nobbs stopped his brief of the butcher's bill and condition of the *Hawk*. "If you are not up to this right now, sir, I can come back at a later time."

Nate shook his head then held it to stop the resulting pain. "That will not be necessary, Simon." He lifted his copy of the report from the desk, glanced through the first few items, then laid it aside and waved his hand for Simon to continue.

Simon cleared his throat. "We have taken twenty-two French and Irish prisoners." He continued as he refreshed his memory from the copy of the report in his hand. "Six are wounded. Doctor Badeau has reported that three of them have mortal wounds and are not expected to live more than two or three days at most."

Nate's eyes glanced up at the mention of the French doctor. "Was the doctor abused while a prisoner?"

"He and the other loyalist were kept chained below with little food or water." Simon replied and waited as Nate watched Jasper fill his glass with rum and water.

"Was the boy harmed?" Nate asked as he stared up at Jasper's passive, black face as his servant dribbled the last of the liquid in his glass. His eyes narrowed and he rubbed his sore head, remembering the last moments before he was clubbed.

Jasper smiled down at his captain. "Will dat be all, sah?"

Nate waved Jasper away with a flip of the hand, and looked back for Simon to continue the report, then watched the departing Jasper as the memory briefly returned.

"We have captured the *Royaliste* and ten of her pirate crew." Simon concluded the report and studied Nate's troubled face.

"Very well, Simon." Nate pulled a blank piece of paper from the stack on his desk and dipped his quill in the ink well, then let the excess ink drip off before beginning to write. "I'll give you these orders in writing to make them official."

"I don't need written orders from you, sir." Simon assured Captain Beauchamp.

"We will both be better served with these orders in writing, Simon." Nate dipped the quill again and this time tapped off the excess ink. "I am sending you and the *Drake* to take the prisoners to the governor in Nassau."

"But Nate I would rather support you in the Florida Keys." Simon pleaded to be included in the coming action against the rebels and pirates.

"I appreciate your eagerness to contribute, Simon, however, we simply cannot take these prisoners with us." Nate watched Simon's reaction.

"We could put them ashore with a small guard, sir," Simon suggested.

Nate slid back in his seat and looked Simon in the eyes. "We cannot afford to leave even a small guard for them." He tapped the end of the quill on the edge of the desk. "We will need all our men for Matecombe Key, besides, if they were to escape it would be hell to pay for the settlers on Rum Cay; none would be safe."

"Of course you are correct, captain." The disappointed Captain Nobbs dropped his head to stare at his boots.

"I need you to personally deliver a letter to the governor and explain our mission to stop the Irish rebels and pirates from salvaging the *San Pedro's* treasure." Nate sprinkled sand over Simon's orders to dry the wet ink, then pulled another piece of paper from the stack and began writing his report to the governor of the Bahama Islands.

"Very well, sir, I will do my best," promised Simon half-heartedly smiling.

"I know you will, Simon." Nate returned Simon's smile.

*****

Nate watched Simon close the cabin door, then turned to the noise coming from the pantry. “Jasper come here a moment.”

The little back man squeezed his head past the pantry door opening. “Yah, sir?”

Captain Beauchamp waved him over. “Come sit down a minute, we need to talk.

Jasper timidly slipped from the pantry and slid easily into the chair Nate pointed to.

“You struck me, did you not?” Nate slightly raised his voice.

“Yah, sah, I did.” Jasper’s black eyes stared at his captain’s green eyes. Not a defiant stare but a stare of a caring friend.

“Do you know you could be flogged or even hanged for striking one of his majesty’s officer’s?” Nate raised his voice louder.

“Yah, sah, I knows.” The little man lowered his head and looked at his open hands that had held the belaying pin.

“Then why in the name of God did you strike me?” Nate demanded.

“I couldn’t let you kill dat woman, sah.” Jasper leaned forward in the chair to stress his point.

“What makes you think I was going to kill Miss Hayes?” Nate too leaned forward, almost meeting the little man at the center of the desk.

“Yah said ya was gonna kill her if’d she don’t sahrenda and she not da kind ta sahrenda, sah.” Jasper eased backward slightly, not giving too much ground but not challenging the captain either.

"What if I did kill her?" Nate almost yelled. "She is an enemy of our king."

Keeping his voice low and even Jasper explained, "Yah, sir, she is but, you got feel'ns fer her and you would be sorry da rest o yor days."

Nate sat back in his chair, quiet for a few seconds, then weakly smiled but never admitted Jasper may be correct about his feelings for the Irish redhead. "Next time let's talk before you decide to club me for my own good." Standing he walked to the water basin and splashed water on his face. "What are you waiting for? Get my supper."

Jumping up, Jasper shuffled off to the pantry with a little sigh of relief.

Nate leaned back to look in the pantry. "And I don't want any of those chitterling things, either!"

Jasper stuck his grinning face half way out of the pantry. "Is yo sho about dem chit'lins, Captain?"

Nate finished drying his face and hands, walked over and placed a reassuring hand on Jasper's shoulder. "No chit'lins, Jasper, and thank you for leaving the clues that led us to Rum Cay."

"I told ya I be learn'n things from that Mr. cola...cola...dat teacher feller." Jasper's grin spread from ear to ear.

*****

Hawk's bow rose as she rode over the flowing swells north of the Cuban coast. She sailed on a westward track toward the Gulf Stream. The powerful flow of water between Cuba and Florida would carry her north through the Straits of Florida and on to the Florida Keys where Matecombe Key and Indian Key sheltered the Irish Rebels and pirates as they salvaged the wreck of the *San Pedro*.

The first few days of the voyage were spent changing the appearance of the pirate ship, *Royaliste*. A few slight changes to her rigging and a coat of black paint to her hull, with the addition of a bright yellow band around her middle at the gun ports.

It was thought that the disguise would make her unrecognizable to even the pirate, Black Caesar. Captain Beauchamp placed Duncan MacKensie as her new master and sent the *Royaliste* ahead to scout Matecumbe Key.

The slower *Hawk* and chase-maree followed and waited for MacKensie and the *Royaliste* to return.

*****

Nate watched the two midshipmen, Daniel Edwards and Pierre Bouchard, talking on the foc'sle and smiled at the young officers. *They are reunited again after Bouchard's imprisonment and Edward's marooning. A few short weeks ago they were mere boys, frolicking around the decks and up and down the shrouds like monkeys.* He glanced eastward, over the ship's transom to the where Fiddler's Island lay below the horizon. *Monkeys, I wonder how Mr. Addington fares on his new island home?*

"Captain," called Master McClain as he approached.

Captain Beauchamp watched the ship's master walk over from the chart table. Taking the offered paper from Mr. McClain's outstretched hand, he read the ship's position. "Looks like we will arrive off Matecombe tomorrow morning, Mr. McClain."

"Aye, sir." McClain stretched his neck to scan the horizon forward of the *Hawk's* bow. "Mr. MacKensie should have reported by now, sir."

Nate glanced forward, following the master's gaze, then up to watch the sun beginning its dip toward the west. "We have a few more hours of light before night." He grinned at the concerned master. "He will report before we arrive at Matecombe, of that I am sure, Mr. McClain."

Both men turned at the sound of footsteps coming up the quarterdeck ladder. Abe Kent buttoned his collar as he strode across the deck to join the captain and the master. Abe lifted his hat, then stated, "I am ready to relieve your watch, sir."

"Very well, Mr. Kent." Nate replied, lifting his bicorn hat in return. "I stand relieved, sir. She sails well with a good current from the Gulf Stream." He glanced aft to see Shell Levy lift his hat from the fok'sle of the chase-maree. He lifted his hat in return and watched Abe read his notes on the *Hawk's* slate hanging next to the binnacle.

Abe called across the deck, over the rattle of the wind worked rigging. "We are getting very close to our destination, sir."

Captain Beauchamp nodded, then looked up as the lookout yelled. "Sail on the larboard quarter." Then before Nate could ask, Mantell yelled once more. "Looks like our pirate ship, your honor."

Major Scarlet appeared at Nate's side. "'Bout bloody time!"

"You colonists certainly have a way with words." Nate grinned at the major.

"Loyalist, sir, through and through." Scarlet waved his arm at the men going about their duties on the main deck and in the rigging. "And just as British as any of these lads."

The captain smiled at the major's antics knowing that many of the remaining crew was foreigners by birth. He spoke to Mr. Kent as he passed by on his way below. "I am going below to freshen up a bit. Bring Captain MacKensie below as soon as his comes aboard, Mr. Kent."

*****

"Sorry it has taken us so long to get back, Captain Beauchamp, sir." Duncan MacKensie swirled his index finger above the seaward side of the islands on Nate's chart of the Florida Straits and the islands that made up the Keys. "We have been dodging a large Spanish frigate these past two days."

Nate rolled his eyes upward to watch Duncan's face as he reported. "What is the situation at the *San Pedro*? Were you able to have a look?"

"The Irish ship is anchored here." Duncan indicated a spot on the chart south of Indian Key. "I believe the waters inshore are too shallow for her." He placed his finger north of Indian Key then ran it west past Lower Matecombe Key. "We ran through this channel to escape the frigate." He glanced at Captain Beauchamp to assure he was following his story. "The Spaniard seems to be protecting the Irish and pirates. We used this shallow channel to escape her."

"Could you see any activity at the wreck site?" Nate queried.

"Yes, sir." Duncan took Nate's quill, gave it a quick dip in the ink well and placed a mark east of Lower Matecumbe Key. "There are two small local craft anchored here." Wiping his brow, he stepped back. "There appears to be plenty of activity at the *San Pedro* site."

Nate stroked his chin. "We have to figure how to get past the frigate, destroy the *Castle Bar* and the local salvage craft." He walked to the aft cabin windows. "And escape with our lives."

*****

Hawk slipped quietly through the darkness sailing slowly toward the lights of the anchored Irish rebel ship *Castle Bar*. Lieutenant Shell

Levy stood the chase-maree off shore, just east of Alligator Reef. Lieutenant Duncan MacKensie sailed the *Royaliste* down the Indian Key Channel on his assigned mission to attack the local craft at the *San Pedro* shipwreck. The British ships were two hours into the attack on the Irish and pirates; too late to retreat from Nathan Beauchamp's plan, so the ships glided on through the darkness.

Gun crews stood silently at their guns. Shirts had been removed and heads and ears wrapped to deaden the sound of the great guns. Gun captains stood at the ready with slow match smoldering, ready for the order to fire the guns. Master Gunner Marcel Folliot's mate tended the armory while the former French Royal Artillery captain walked along an invisible line behind his gun crews on the lower deck. Lieutenant Foster grinned at Midshipman Bouchard when the gunner passed them in his former artillery uniform.

Bouchard leaned toward Foster and whispered. "He thinks he will die today and would rather die as a French Royalist than a British seaman."

Foster watched the old man walk down the line of canon talking to a gun captain here, then a pat on the back and a word of encouragement to a seaman there. Foster nodded to the young midshipman. "Many of us may die today, my friend."

On the main deck it was much the same for the men standing at their stations. The only difference was that these men could watch as they drew near the lights of the Irish ship. A fish splashed beside the ship and startled the tense seamen. Once it was realized the sudden noise was a fish the men grinned at each other. The tension relieved for a few moments.

Nate watched the lights draw near and glanced seaward, checking the horizon for the Spanish frigate. The horizon revealed nothing but darkness.

"*Castle Bar*, strange name for a ship," Midshipman Edwards wondered aloud.

The *Hawk's* captain listened as Sergeant Major Thomas Christmas explained the name to the young midshipman. "Not so strange a name for Irish Rebels to give their ship, if you know a little bit of the struggle we faced during the rebellion in '98." Christmas wet his lips and continued telling his story. "Back in '98, 1500 French and Irish troops attacked our garrison at *Castle Bar* in North West Ireland. They drove our troops out of the town capturing eleven big guns and all our supplies." He lowered his head. "It was one of the worse defeats our troops have ever endured."

Daniel Edwards stared at the *Castle Bar's* lights. "I did not know."

Hawk turned to bring her broadsides to bear and sailed to obtain the position to fire.

"Sir," Lieutenant Kent called to his captain. "I thought I heard something off the larboard side."

They moved silently to the rail and scanned the darkness, listening and watching for a sign, any sign, of an enemy while the *Hawk* obtained her station to fire. Suddenly the darkness flashed with the light of canon. The magnitude of the flash could only be the flash of a frigate's canon firing in unison.

"Get down, get down!" Kent and Beauchamp yelled to the crew together as they dove for the safety of the deck.

Canon balls ripped through the *Hawk's* sides, ripping the bulwark and rigging. Spars and blocks rained down on the men waiting at their guns. Splinters ripped through the British seamen, cutting down many of them.

Nate and Abe Kent jumped to their feet to look through the carnage on the deck of the *Hawk* and at the men remaining at the guns.

"That ship is close!" Kent screamed over the moaning of the wounded seamen. "The *Hawk* was not built to withstand a pounding like this." He glanced to the carnage on the main deck. "We are going to be ripped to pieces."

Captain Beauchamp glanced to where the frigate had fired then to the activity on the deck of the *Castle Bar*. He saw the red hair of Barbara Hayes on the ship's quarterdeck. His heart pained at what he must do, he had come too far to not complete his mission. The Irish must be stopped from funding their revolution. He yelled at the master gunner who had stuck his head up the ladder to the lower deck. "Mr. Folliot, fire what guns you can at the Irish ship."

The master gunner, in the splendor of his Royal French Artillery officer's uniform, saluted the captain and ran back down the ladder to the lower gun deck.

Lieutenant Kent rushed to the main deck guns, rounding up able men as he went. Soon he was able to man most of the guns of the starboard battery. He looked up to Nate on the quarterdeck and fired when Nate nodded.

The *Hawk's* single broadside, aimed at her hull, was more than the Irish merchant ship could stand. Smoke billowed up her hatches and she tilted over taking water over her larboard side. The smoke cleared to show longboats pulling around the ship's sinking hull bound for the shore of Lower Matecombe Key.

Lieutenant Kent rushed to the quarterdeck. "There is a fire below that we can not get out, sir." Kent glanced down the ladder to the lower deck. "I don't know what will take her first, the fire or the water rushing through the hole in her side." He grasped Nate's arm. "The *Hawk* is sinking, Captain."

Nate continued to stare at the departing Irish longboats, trying to see if Barbara was on one of them but they disappeared into the dark before he could find her. He turned back to the waiting first officer. "Get the as many boats in the water as you can before she goes down."

"Capt'n." Jasper called as he ran up the quarterdeck ladder; reaching out a watertight pouch.

Captain Beauchamp took the pouch. "Are all the logs in here, Jasper?"

A great grinding noise came across the waters from the darkness where the Spanish frigate was sailing. Then a sound of crashing rigging rang across the water.

"She has struck the reef!" Abe shouted. The seamen cheered, then at the urging of Mr. Papas, they climbed down the side of the ship to the waiting boats.

"She should have been under reduced sail like the *Hawk* was." Nate looked around at his wrecked and sinking ship. Black smoke billowed up the open hatches while the fire lapped at the upper deck from the lower deck. Soon the fire would spread to the upper deck and rigging. Nate stood in a trance at the starboard rail watching the flashes of the *Royaliste's* guns as she sailed in to destroy the local craft at the salvage site. *At least we have stopped them for now.*

"Come now, captain," Lieutenant Kent called from the entry port. "She won't stay afloat much longer."

Nate moved down the quarterdeck ladder as he listened to the screams coming from the Spanish frigate. "They are more frightened than harmed," he told Kent as he reached the entry port. "They hit the reef pretty hard but she should not sink, most of the bottom around here is sand." He stared into the darkness as he started down the ladder to his waiting gig. "They should be able to float her on the next tide and will have a jury rig on her in a few days." Stepping back to his seat in the stern of the gig he handed the ship's log pouch back to Jasper to hold. "This won't be a good place for us to linger for too long." The gig pulled away from *Hawk's* side and stood off in the dark. The gig cleared the *Hawk* to a safe distance, then they turned back to look at their sinking ship. The lights on the Spanish frigate silhouetted the *Hawk*.

The gig lay hove too while they watched the smoldering *Hawk* slowly sink below the surface.

Master Ezra McClain wiped his eyes with the back of his hand. "I guess she were an honorable ship after all," he said, speaking to no one in particular.

"That she was Mr. McClain, that she was." Nate turned to the coxswain and motioned him to row towards the *Royaliste.*

Chapter Eleven

Nassau

The governor sat his glass next to his empty diner plate. "Quite a story, Commander. There will be an inquiry into the loss of the *Hawk* and perhaps a court martial." He sat his glass on the edge of the table and motioned for the black servant to refill his glass and then motioned the man to Nate's empty glass.

Nate slid the glass across the tablecloth and watched as the liquid trickled slowly into the glass. "Yes, sir, I anticipated such actions." He sipped the claret then sat the glass next to his half eaten dinner. "It is not everyday a captain looses one of his majesty's ships."

"What of the Irish who escaped the *Castle Bar*?" The governor slid his chair back and motioned to the tobacco box and a pair of pipes on the mantel.

Nate waved off the offered pipe and tobacco. "When daylight came we were picked up by

Lieutenant Levy in the chase-maree, then sailed through the shallows to meet with Lieutenant MacKensie and the *Royaliste.*" He sipped at the claret once more then continued. "We searched Lower Matecumbe and the surrounding islands but never found any sign of the Irish nor the pirates." Nate took a deep breath. "They must have had another shallow draught vessel on the other side of the island." He stood when the governor did and they walked into the governor's garden. "We searched for a few days, then gave up finding them and sailed here.

The governor turned as it reoccurred to him that he had a message for Nate. "There is an Admiralty officer here who wishes to speak with you." The governor walked to his garden pond as he talked. "Some kind of cloak and dagger chap." He placed his forefinger on his chin attempting to remember the man's name. "Oh yes, a Commodore Culleton, said for you to meet him at the White Lion Inn this evening at nine o'clock."

Nate pulled his watch from his waistcoat pocket and stared at the portrait of Virginia Crampton and then the time. "That is only and hour away, I should take my leave now, sir."

They walked back to the dining room. "Very well, Commander, and I do wish you luck with the inquiry."

"Thank you, sir." Nate retrieved his hat and made for the front door.

*****

Light raindrops thumped the taunt, blackened, canvas roof of the governor's carriage as it slowly moved along the back streets of Nassau. Nathan Beauchamp pulled at the ill-fitting waistcoat borrowed from the governor's secretary. The governor was correct in suggesting a naval uniform is not attire one would wear to a clandestine meeting in Nassau's Harbor District.

The rain increased its tattoo on the roof as the carriage increased speed to pass a slow moving peddler's cart, then the burly black driver turned onto Bay Street. Nate suspected the driver to be more than he seemed as he was well armed and seldom far from the governor. Perhaps William, as the governor called him, was the governor's protector.

William stopped the carriage, to the disappointment of the governor's matched white horses, across from the corner of Fowler Street and opened the door for Nate to exit the carriage. Nate stepped out and pulled at the borrowed waistcoat. The governor's secretary's build was slightly less than Nate's and the waistcoat kept riding up, requiring constant adjustments. "High strung horses are they not?" he asked the tall black man.

"All a matter of breeding, sir," William replied.

Nate studied William's face in the glair of light from the busy shops across the street. Three straight, raised lines crossed William's cheeks just below each eye; some sort of tribal tattoo Nate surmised. William's speech was not the accent one would expect of a black slave in this part of the world. His accent was just as British as his own, though he was unable to detect which district of England it favored. "Yes, breeding has much to do with one's demeanor and actions, I suppose."

William raised his tree trunk like arms and pointed across Bay Street toward Fowler Street. "You will fine the White Lion in the third alleyway on the left, sir." Nate followed William's arm, then turned back to watch as William climbed up to the carriage's driver seat with never another word. He snapped the whip over the fidgeting horses and sped the carriage away.

Nate glanced at the anchored ship lights dotting Nassau Bay and the light of businesses and homes on Paradise Island half a mile across the bay. He paid particular attention to where the *Royaliste* lay at anchor awaiting the government survey to determine if she would be taken into the service as one of His Majesty's war ships.

The commander, in his borrowed civilian clothes, crossed Bay Street and walked through the maze of people moving up and down Fowler Street. No one took notice of what appeared to be a clerk out on a stroll in this busy seaport. He turned down the third alley and shortly found the small weathered sign identifying the White Lion Inn. Pulling the door open, he stepped into the noisy and smoke-filled tavern. The heat from the candles and lanterns coupled with the body heat of the mass of patrons caused him to pull at his waistcoat then flap the lapels of the frocked topcoat while he looked around the benches and tables for the familiar face of Commodore Culleton.

A tall bosomy auburn haired woman touched his arm. Being on King's business and having no current interest in what women in these places usually had to offer, he pulled his arm to his side and out of reach of the lovely woman.

She leaned into him, pinning him against a stanchion and asked, "Commander Beauchamp?"

Nate stared at the woman for a short time, wondering how she had named him and then nodded.

"Follow me." She tugged on his lapel, then shoved her way through the throng of customers. Nate followed her to a group of booths at the back of the tavern. They stopped at a booth where a tall black haired man sat with his back to him. The man stood as soon as the woman stopped at his booth. She pointed to Nate and the man turned around and immediately smiled and extended his hand. "Good to see you again, Mr. Brown." Commodore Culleton glanced around the adjoining tables to determine if the other patrons took notice. He pointed to the bench across from his for Nate to take a seat then nodded to the blonde woman. "Thank you, Miss Karen, I am indebted to you."

Miss Karen took the commodore's hands in hers, rubbing them as she spoke. "Never think of it, Mr. Stevens, weren't no problem at all."

She smiled and returned to the front of the tavern and her place near the bar. Nate watched her sway as she moved away and made a mental note to return to the White Lion at some time in the future.

Commodore Culleton leaned across the table and lowered his voice. "Commander, I need you for a mission which may endanger your naval career and possibly your life. If you fail, it may mean the end of the British Union as we know it." The commodore scanned the tavern to see if they were being watched. Then turned back to the commander and reached a sealed pouch across the table. "I am asking you to place your reputation in jeopardy. I'm asking you to run, to desert, to become a rogue officer," the commodore glanced over his shoulder then lowered his voice once more leaning closer to the young commander, "I need you to become a pirate for your King."

"Sir, I just completed an assignment similar to that and I look forward to returning to England and my family." The young commander forcefully exclaimed.

"Mr. Brown, need I remind you that the sugar you were to obtain for us was never brought to the warehouse." Commodore Culleton disguised his words to conceal their meaning from those within hearing.

Commander Beauchamp wrinkled his brow, wondering what was the meaning of the commodore's strange statement.

Culleton tried a different tact to convey his meaning to Commander Beauchamp. "That sugar shipment could be sailing around the Caribbean to who knows where."

Beauchamp realized the commodore was talking about his failure to capture or kill the Hayes siblings. "Oh! Yes, Mr. Stevens, that is true." Nate stroked his chin. "I suppose I do owe an obligation to retrieve that shipment."

The commodore stood and extended his hand to the young commander. "Good, Mr. Brown, I will expect some action to retrieve the shipment in the near future." Commodore Culleton glanced at the pouch laying next to Nate's elbow, then walked to the tavern door where he glance at the woman before passing through the front door.

Nate looked over to the woman the commodore had called Miss Karen. She smiled back at him with a knowing look. *Is she one of the commodore's operatives? If so, perhaps I can use her to inform Commodore Culleton of my suspicions about Commodore Fry's involvement in the Irish revolution.*

*****

Nathan Beauchamp had spent the remainder of the night reviewing the papers in the pouch given to him by Commodore Culleton. The Hayes siblings had escaped him at Matecombe Key and changed from recovering Spanish treasure to piracy. Black Caesar helped Tom Hayes steal an armed schooner from Key West and now he and his sisters, Barbara and Christina, were attacking ships of all nations. Their trail of successful attacks moved from Florida, southward across the Caribbean. A direction that would lead one to believe they were leaving the area and moving toward the South American Atlantic coast.

Nate leafed through the stack of papers to his official orders. He pulled the orders from the stack and reviewed them once again. *I am to become a deserter. What will mother and my brothers' think?* He laid the orders down then pulled a stack of signed, blank pardons for any King's man who would join him in this ruse to capture the Hayes family.

He laid down the pardons and walked to the window over looking Nassau Bay. *I'm to steal a ship and man her with British tars without getting captured by the King's Navy.* He absent-mindedly looked out the window to where the sun seemed to be shining on the seventy-four-gun ship *Maestro* and her captain, Sir James Goddard.

Nate remembered hearing of Captain Goddard as a by-the-book senior captain with the tenacity of a bulldog once he set himself and his ship to a task. He leaned on the window frame scanning the harbor for a fast ship to fill the requirements of his orders. *I need something to out sail a seventy-four, yet with enough firepower to stop the Irish rebels from gaining enough wealth to fund the rebellion.* His eyes came to rest on the *Royaliste. Shallow draft to get in among the islands, armed well and fast enough to escape a British seventy-four with the right wind and plenty of shallow water between Nassau and the Caribbean.*

"Jasper, send for Mr. Levy." Nate smiled as he sent for the perfect officer to join his venture. *How can he say no? With independent duty, no senior officers to report to and plenty of adventures.* He laughed out loud to the empty room. *That is, if we survive to clear our names.*

Glossary of Nautical Terms

Abreast - The situation of two or more ships lying with their sides parallel, and their heads equally advanced; in which case they are abreast of each other.

Aft - Behind, or near the stern of the ship.

A-ground - The situation of a ship when her bottom, or any part of it, rests in the underwater ground.

A-head - Any thing which is situated forward of the ship.

Aloft - At the mast heads, or any where about the higher rigging.

Along side - Side by side, or joined to a ship, wharf &c.

Amidships - The middle of a ship, either with regard to her length or breadth.

To anchor - To let the anchor fall into the ground, for the ship to ride thereby.

Anchorage - underwater ground fit to hold a ship by her anchor.

At anchor - The situation of a ship riding at her anchor.

Astern - Any distance behind a ship, as opposed to A-HEAD.

Athwart - Across the line of a ship's course or keel.

Athwart-ships - A direction across the ship from one side to the other.

Bay - Water sheltered by land for ships to anchor.

Ballast - Is either pigs of iron, stones, or gravel, which last is called single ballast; and their use is to bring the ship down to her bearings in the water which her provisions and stores will not do. Trim the ballast, that is spread it about and lay it even, or run over one side of the hold to the other.

Between decks - The space contained between any two decks of a ship.

Bilge - The lower part of the ship, usually contains a collection of water seepage.

Binnacle - A kind of box to contain the compasses in upon the deck.

Birth - The station in which a ship rides at anchor, either alone, or in a fleet; the due distance between two ships; and also a room or apartment for the officers of a mess.

Block - A piece of wood with running sheaves or wheels in it, through which the running rigging is passed, to add to the purchase.

To board a ship - To enter an enemy's ship in an engagement.

Bowsprit - A large piece of timber which stands out from the bows of a ship.

Broadside - A discharge of all the guns on one side of a ship both above and bellow.

Bulwark - The sides of a ship above the decks.

Capstan - An instrument by which the anchor is weighed out of the ground, it being a great mechanical power, and is used for setting up the shrouds, and other work where great purchases are required.

Chase - A vessel pursued by some other.

Chaser - The vessel pursuing.

Dunnage - A quantity of loose wood, &c. laid at the bottom of a ship to keep the goods from being damaged. Often seamen's personal belongings are referred to as dunnage.

Flood-tide - The state of a tide when it flows or rises to full depth.

Fore - That part of a ship that lies near the stem.

Fore-and-aft - Throughout the whole ship's length. Lengthways of the ship.

Forecastle (Fok'sl) - The upper deck in the fore part of the ship.

Forward - Towards the fore part of a ship.

Grounding - The laying a ship a-shore, in order to repair her. It is also applied to running a-ground accidentally.

Gunroom - A division of the lower deck, abaft, enclosed with network, for the use of the gunner and junior lieutenant, and in which their cabins stand.

Halyards - The ropes by which the sails are hoisted, as the topsail halyards, the jib halyards, &c.

Harbor - A secure place for a ship to anchor.

Hawse - The situation of the cables before the ship's stem, when she is moored with two anchors out from forwards. It also denotes any small distance a-head of a ship, or the space between her head and the anchors employed to ride her.

Hawse-holes - The holes in the bows of the ship through which the cables pass. Freshen hawse, veer out more cable. Clap a service in the hawse, put somewhat round the cable in the hawse hole to prevent its chafing. To clear hawse, is to untwist the cables where the ship is moored, and has got a foul hawse. Athwart hawse is to be across or before another ship's head.

To heel - To stoop or incline to one side; thus they say TO HEEL TO PORT; that is, to heel to the larboard side.

Helm - The instrument by which the ship is steered, and includes both the wheel and the tiller, as one general term.

To hoist - To draw up any body by the assistance of one or more tackles. Pulling by means of a single block is never termed HOISTING, except only the drawing of the sails upwards along the masts or stays.

Hold - Is the space between the lower deck and the bottom of a ship and where her stores, &c. lie. To stow the hold, is to place the things in it.

Hoy - A particular kind of vessel used for taking supplies from the shore to a ship. Today's term is barge.

Hull of the ship - The body of it.

To hull a ship - To fire cannon-balls into her hull.

Hulk - A ship without masts or rigging; also a vessel to remove masts into or out of ships by means of sheers, from whence they are called sheer hulks.

Juryrig - Any spar that is set up, to be used as a mast when the proper mast is carried away.

Knot - A division of the knot-line, answering, in the calculation of the ship's velocity, to one mile.

Larboard - The left side of a ship, looking towards the head.

Larboard-tack - The situation of a ship when sailing with the wind blowing upon her larboard side.

Lash - To bind.

To leak - When water comes into the hull through breaches in the sides or bottom.

Look-out - A person assigned, usually atop a spar on a mast, to watch the surrounding seas for ships, land wreckage, etc.

Magazine - A place where gunpowder is kept.

To make sail - To increase the quantity of sail already set, either by unreefing, or by setting others.

Masts - The upright spars on which the yards and sails are set.

Mooring - Securing a ship in a particular station by chains or cables, which are either fastened to an adjacent shore, or to anchors at the bottom.

Muster - To assemble.

Oakum - Old rope untwisted and pulled open.

Oars - What boats are rowed with.

On board - with in the ship; as, he is come on board.

Orlop - The deck on which the cables are stowed.

Over-board - Out of the ship; as in, he fell overboard, meaning he fell out of, or from, the ship

Pendant - The long narrow flag worn at the mast-head by all ships of the royal navy. Brace pendants are those ropes which secure the brace-blocks to the yard-arms.

Pendant broad - A broad pendant hoisted by a commodore

Quarters - The several stations of a ship's crew in time of action.

To rake - To cannonade a ship at the stern or head, so that the balls scour the whole length of the decks.

Ratlines - The small ropes fastened to the shrouds, by which the men go aloft.

Rudder - The machine by which the ship is steered.

Salvage - A part of the value of a ship and cargo paid to the salvos.

Seams - The joints between the planks.

To set sail - To unfurl and expand the sails to the wind, in order to give motion to the ship.

To ship - To take any person, goods, or things, on board. It also implies to fix any thing in its proper place; as, to SHIP THE OARS, to fix them in their rowlocks.

Spars - Pieces of trees as they are cut in the wood.

Starboard - The right-hand side of the ship, when looking forward.

Starboard-tack - A ship is said to be on the STARBOARD-TACK when sailing with the wind blowing upon her starboard side.

Stem - The fore-part of the vessel.

Stern - The after-part of a vessel.

Tarpaulin - A cloth of canvas covered with tar and saw-dust, or some other composition, so as to make it water-proof.

Tiller - A large piece of wood, or beam, put into the head of the rudder, and by means of which the rudder is moved.

Transom - A large piece of timber fastened to the stern-posts, to the ends of which the after-part of the bends are fastened.

To trim the sails - To dispose the sails in the best arrangement for the course which a ship is steering.

Under- way - When a ship is loosened from moorings, and is under the government of her sails and rudder.

Wake - The path or track impressed on the water by the ship's passing through it, leaving a smoothness in the sea behind it. A ship is said to come into the wake of another when she follows her in the same track, and is chiefly done in bringing ships to, or in forming the line of battle.

To weigh anchor - To heave up an anchor from the bottom.

Weigh - To haul up; as, weigh the anchor.

Yards - The timbers upon which the sails are spread.

This glossary is compiled from various nautical Internet reference data and lists common used age of sail terminology that are considered public domain.

About The Author

Joseph L. O'Steen was born February 16, 1950 in Jacksonville, Florida. He started life as the son of a commercial fisherman. His father first took him to sea at age four, and he spent his early youth on the shrimping grounds of St. Augustine, Cape Canaveral and Key West, Florida. Usually the fishing boats only went to sea in good weather, but one trip caught the boat on the edge of a hurricane. The adults were frightened but for a seven year old, tied in the wheelhouse chair, riding the 30-foot waves and sliding downward into the trough between the waves was like a carnival ride. The happiest times of Joseph's childhood were on those trips to the fishing grounds.

Joseph was adopted at age eleven and settled into a life ashore. His love of the sea never died. He visited the local docks and talked to the fishermen almost every day. Joseph read as many nautical books as he could get his hands on and watched every movie about the sea, from pirates and age of sail, to the modern stories of World War 2. His heroes were the great ships and the men who sailed them. Eventually the call of the sea was too strong to resist and Joseph ran away from home in his senior year of high school to join the U. S. Navy.

After having spent two enlistments in the Navy where he completed seven progressively advanced Navy schools from basic seamanship through Nondestructive Testing, Joseph obtained his high school GED, as well as a few collage credits while working his way up to First Class Petty Officer. Joseph spent two cruises on the aircraft carrier John F. Kennedy that took him to the Atlantic Ocean, the North Sea, the Mediterranean and Caribbean Sea. He visited ports steeped in nautical history in France, Spain, Italy, Greece, Turkey, Scotland, and Jamaica.

When he returned home to St. Augustine with his growing family, Joseph found a changed and dwindling fishing industry with no need for a twenty-seven year old man with family responsibilities who had been too long out of the business. Using his Navy training, he went to work at the local aircraft factory. Soon, he discovered a knack for writing technical proposals, factory capabilities books, corporate policies/procedures and a few employee position descriptions. He has achieved positions as Inspection Manager, Industrial Engineering Supervisor, Advance Planner and Facilities Planning Supervisor.

Joseph never lost his love of the sea and sea stories and has read all of C. S. Forester, Patrick O'Brien, Alexander Kent, Dudley Pope and dozens of other author's sea stories. He read so many books, so fast, that they could not be published fast enough for his hunger. He waited impatiently for months for the latest book to be published.

Joseph's wife, Chris, persuaded him to write his own sea stories while waiting for Alexander Kent's *Second to None* to be published. Joseph started writing as a naval officer at the Hart of Oaks role-playing site online, where he created Nathan Beauchamp, a British Naval officer in 1803. Soon the role-playing was not enough, so he researched British naval histories and started to write the Nathan Beauchamp series.

With his books, Joseph provides the reader with a fast paced, action filled, sea story without the great detail to ship and sail handling found in most books of this genre. His style provides new readers an entry to the much more detailed books of the great authors whose works he loves. Forester, Kent, Pope, Lambdin, Stockwin, O'Brian, White, Nelson and so many more have provided him with many hours of reading pleasure as their protagonists waged war in the age of sail.

The author hopes his readers will enjoy the Nathan Beauchamp series as much as he is enjoying writing them. He welcomes visitors to his website at: http://josephlosteen.com

Printed in the United States
24303LVS00002B/1-54